Salvage

The God Stripe Saga

Denny Connolly

Copyright © 2025 by Denny Connolly

All rights reserved.

No part of this book may be reproduced in any form or by any electronic or mechanical means, including information storage and retrieval systems, without written permission from the author, except for the use of brief quotations in a book review.

The story, all names, characters, and incidents portrayed in this production are fictitious. No identification with actual persons (living or deceased), places, buildings, and products is intended or should be inferred.

Book cover and illustrations by Chris Olds.

ISBN: 979-8-9920495-0-3

epub: 979-8-9920495-1-0

Library of Congress Control Number: 2024924749

For my Family

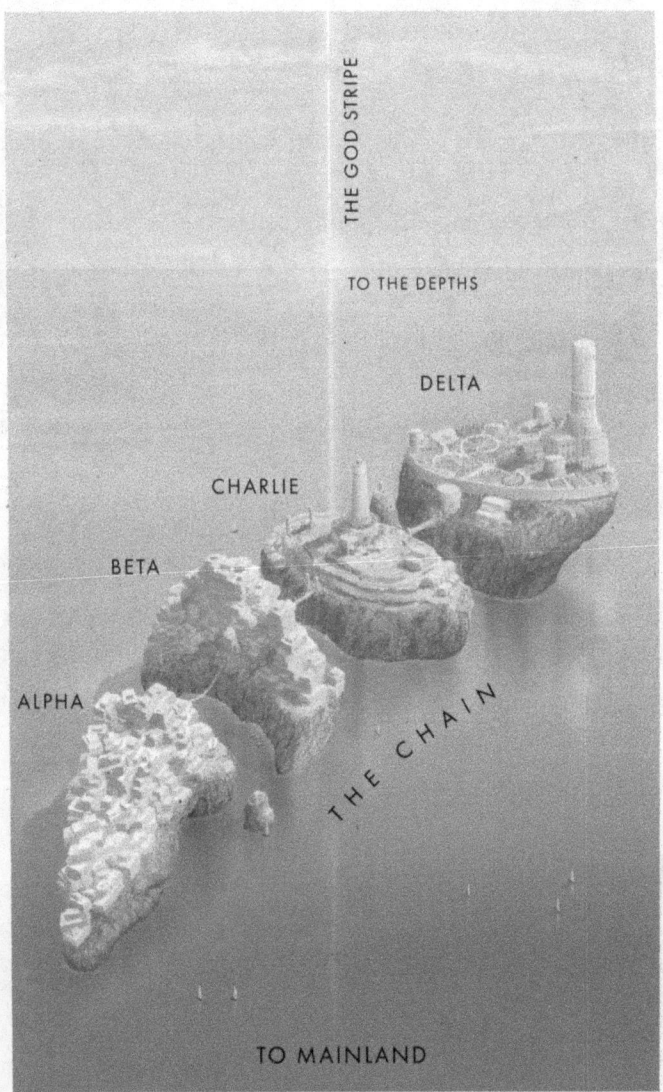

Part One

The Islands

In the years before the Truthbringer, the law of the Baron was the only reality we knew.

—Aphra of Alpha, Colonel of the Truthkeepers

Chapter 1

Beth

When she first returned with the sacred tome, not even the Truthbringer herself knew the cyclones she had set into motion.

—From the journal of Aphra of Alpha, Colonel of the Truthkeepers

Despite the coral spear two inches from her eye and the pair of thugs looming over her in the dark, Beth felt like she had the situation under control. Mitch was quick to point that sharp stick around, but Beth had never actually seen him stab anybody . . . at least, not anybody from their own island.

Beth had a long history of successful jobs with Mitch and his crew, this failed deal and their generous compensation notwithstanding. Although she was born on Alpha, the two had come up together on Beta, the second lowest of the four towering islands. On the Chain, birth island determined just about everything. Alpha and Beta born citizens grew up in overcrowded stacks, following the laws that the Baron handed down from her tower up on Delta. The snobs on Charlie weren't royalty the same way that those on Delta were, but they might as well be for how they looked down on the lower islands. The criminal underbelly of the Chain was only so big. Beth's business partner and closest friend, Portia, grew up on Beta and lived in the same housing stack as Mitch. Frequent visits with Portia's family is what made Beth more of a child of Beta than her home island of Alpha.

The current job had started off fine. And it actually ended fine. Beth and Toby, one of Mitch's henchmen, snuck up to the Chain's third island, Charlie, and made off with some contraband produce. Or was this the job with Dale? She always got those two confused. Mitch's underlings didn't have the personality to leave much of an impression. Anyway . . . Beth had subtly moved the fruit and spices through Portia's corner store and split the profits with Mitch. That's where things fell apart.

In exchange for the stolen harvest—which was heretical to even *have* on Beta—a regular at the store offered Beth two full barrels of sea debris he had managed to skim off the ocean surface after a recent storm. Yet another case of heresy. The contraband debris could be used for all kinds of things and, in Beth's mind, held infinite value. In the right hands, the solid pieces could be used to build small gardening structures, weapons, and who knows what else. Even the stacks themselves that towered into the skies and provided housing on the lower islands were made out of much larger pieces of that same sea debris. The material was white and looked like it could've been spit up out of the depths by giant monsters who were rotting away deep under the violent sea. Low islanders called those larger chunks sea bones. Despite the resemblance to imagined monster bones, the sea scraps weren't organic and clearly seemed man made in nature to Beth and Portia. That theory didn't follow the scripture that the upper islands enforced. According to the know-it-alls on Charlie and Delta, the sea scraps were gifts from the God Stripe, sent down from the heavens for the Baron to distribute at her discretion. Or, more often, to keep for herself and the rest of the rich.

Despite their scarcity, not everyone shared Beth's enthusiasm for the sea scraps. Mitch couldn't wrap his head around the raw potential in the barrel he had just knocked over in the middle of his fit.

"Credits. Herbs. Rations. *Any* of those would be normal payments, Beth. I've told you a thousand times, I'm not interested in your striping sea scraps." Despite his wiry frame and handsome features, he could actually be a little intimidating when he tried.

"Slow down, Mitch. There's *value* in that barrel. Real value."

"You've pulled these stunts—" Mitch raged on, still pointing his coral spear at Beth while she knelt on the dark rooftop of a midsize stack. In the midst of his rant, something other than Mitch's bulging forehead vein and flushed cheeks caught her eye. From Beth's point of view the red projectile streaked across the sky over Mitch's right shoulder. Just below the God Stripe that broke the sky in two overhead, a cluster of red lights raced downward.

The God Stripe was a constant. A bright, white series of lines that could always be spotted somewhere in the skies. Most islanders worshiped it and pointed their prayers up to it in hopes that someday they might ascend to the God Stripe and earn an afterlife in the heavens. Beth wasn't so sure about all of that. It was good for keeping time and navigating on the open seas. She couldn't deny that. And right now the light it provided was perfect for tracking the falling cluster of rocks smashing down from the heavens.

"It's trash, B. It's striping garbage." Mitch concluded.

A smile flashed across Beth's face as the red light flared in her dark brown eyes.

"You say that like it's a bad thing."

Mitch caught the reflection in Beth's eyes and craned his neck toward the skies himself. Toby (or was it Dale?) followed his pal's lead, and for just a moment the whole trio watched as the debris plummeted down closer to their chain of islands. They were all enthralled by the skies above with only the sound of the waves crashing into the base of the island below disturbing the silence. Beth was the first to break her stare when she spotted an opening. She pounced up from her knees, grasping the shaft of Mitch's spear and jamming the handle into his gut. In the blink of an eye, their positions had flip-flopped, and he was the one falling to his knees in pain as Beth pried the spear from his weakened grip and immediately widened her stance in anticipation of an attack from Toby. She was pretty sure he was Toby.

I didn't want to rough up these two, but I can't waste any more time here. Not if I want to reach it first . . .

Just as expected, Toby ran straight for her. Beth smoothly sidestepped out of his path and lowered Mitch's spear into place for a strike to his shins. Toby's face smacked off the rooftop with enough force to make Beth feel a little guilty. As her eyes went back toward the skies to track the trajectory of the falling space rocks, Mitch reached up and grabbed her by the forearm. Instinct kicked in, and she jammed the shaft of the spear into his face with her free hand. Once again, Mitch fell to the ground, this time clutching his nose.

"I'll striping kill you for this, Beth! What's wrong with you?"

The debris broke the tree line inland, and Beth mentally took note of the location. It must've struck the mainland just beyond the swamps. She'd never ventured that far inland before, but it wasn't impossible. If she could survive the swamps, she felt sure she could survive a day's hike on the other side of them too. She could get there. It could be hers. It could be *theirs*.

"Keep the payment, Mitch. Let's call it even."

Chapter 2

Jonah

When our people settled on the islands to escape the dangers of the mainland, the God Stripe rewarded their resolve with gifts from above.

—Excerpt from the departure letter of Lord Drolt, Senior Adviser to Baron Agrius

Jonah's oversized robe kicked up dust as he hurried across Delta's royal courtyard and through the gardens where the Heir often spent her days digging in the soil. This precious ground was sacred. Most of the vegetation on the Chain was farmed and harvested on Charlie, but the gardens in this courtyard were full of crops so rare that those outside of the Delta elite would never hear of their existence, let alone smell their petals or taste their fruits. Though his tread was especially light for a retired templar, he still made enough commotion to send a group of birds darting away from their resting place in a nearby tree. The small flock soared down toward the sea to hunt for an evening meal. Jonah's heel crushed a violet flower and left an imprint in the dirt, but he didn't have the time to stop and say a prayer to the God Stripe for its passing. Not when God Rocks were falling from the heavens.

He rhythmically tapped his fingers on his weathered notebook as he climbed the spiral stairs up to Baron Tamiyo's tower chambers. It was a habit nearly as old as he was; he'd picked up the soothing melody from his older sister ages ago. He would tap along to the beat on his bedpost while she soothed him during the water cyclones. Years later, he proudly tapped out that same beat on his shield during his decades of service, first as a recruit and then as a full templar in the Baron's Honor Guard. And now, even as a graybeard, he still drummed away when things went wrong. And this had *definitely* gone wrong.

"She'll be expecting me." Before the words were out of Jonah's mouth, the pair of guards had stepped aside and shouldered open the heavy door. The ornate floral decorations on the door left it nearly unrecognizable from the sea scraps it was carved from. Repurposing the sea scraps was a criminal offense on the lower islands of the Chain and was a privilege reserved for only those projects that The Baron deemed essential. When the God Stripe offered gifts of sea scraps, they crashed up in the waves at the bases of the Chain. The Baron's Depth Walkers were in charge of retrieving the material and delivering it to Delta, but occasionally some overzealous low islanders beat them to the treasures. A heretical crime punishable by judgment at sea. Despite the severity of that crime, it didn't even begin to compare to what was at stake when God Rocks fell from the skies as they had this night.

Though the guards interacted with Jonah on a daily basis, he still couldn't help but notice the way they avoided eye contact with him. The underlying sense of disappointment as he marched around with his little notebook as his only weapon. They knew where he started, and whether they would admit it or not, they had certainly heard the rumors about how he ended up here.

He strode into the room and addressed Tamiyo, who was tending a small herb garden hanging in the tower's balcony. Most prior Baron's conducted their business in the designated ground-level office in the Citadel, but Tamiyo preferred the view from the heights. She had a desk built in the upper tower and spent most of her waking hours there watering her plants or staring out over the rough waters below. Jonah had worked as the Baron's Senior Adviser for long enough to know she wouldn't appreciate him skirting the topic at hand.

"Did you see it, Your Highness?" he asked.

"Did I see it, Templar Jonah? A gift from the God Stripe falling through the sky at sunset just before curfew? I think it's safe to say the whole striping Chain had a pretty good view, don't you?"

Well, at least she's in a good enough mood to jest . . .

"Very true, your highness. The projected landing site is twenty chains inland. Just a day's hike through the swamps and dust cyclone territory."

Tamiyo plucked a crimson grape from a nearby bowl, sighed, and returned to the plants, turning her back toward Jonah. She gestured with her tattooed arm toward the watering can across the room. Jonah obediently retrieved it.

"And?" Tamiyo questioned without looking up from her work.

"Yes, my lady?"

"Templar Jonah. You're the Senior Adviser to the Throne and have been since the day your Sword of Power was retired, yes?"

Not the career path he had in mind, but here he was anyway. His sword wielding calluses had faded long ago.

"Of course, my lady. Nearly that day, yes." Jonah hoped she wouldn't notice his instinctive flinch as the memories of his final days as a true Templar flashed through his mind.

"Advise me."

Too slow. Always too slow.

Jonah placed the watering can in her outstretched hand and opened his journal to the marked page. "We'll have to send a team out immediately, but we should easily be the first to secure the location without any problems."

"We depths well better. The usual scouting party?" Tamiyo asked.

"No, my lady. That party . . . lost a few too many members in last winter's wyvern expedition. Templar Mullen has a very experienced group of recruits at the ready if you would like to stray from the usual team…"

"I would not." He knew the answer before asking, but he had to try. Anything to avoid more contact with Malcolm than necessary. Or more dead recruits on their hands.

"Right. Of course not. We'll still have Templar Malcolm at the head of the team, but the majority of his recruits are . . . more green than preferred. Particularly for a mission this important."

Tamiyo's gaze left the green leaves and buds hanging in front of her and moved out over the series of islands that lay ahead of her. The Chain. From the height of her tower, she could see all the way down to the messy, uneven stacks of Alpha. The ignorant masses. How easy life must be without the weight of the crown and the God Stripe hanging overhead. The secrets. The lies. On more than one occasion Tamiyo had admitted to Jonah that there were days she was actually jealous of them, though not so jealous that she would give up life on Delta and her private gardens and return to the slums. She reached for another grape and bit into the rare fruit as her eyes drifted upward to the God Stripe. A bright, white band wrapped around the planet like a belt pulled too tight.

"Have them gather in the courtyard before they set sail. Perhaps a send-off from their fearless leader will solidify the importance of their mission." Her waist-length black hair glinted in the reflection of the God Stripe's light bouncing off the ocean water below as she turned to face Jonah.

"Right away, my lady."

Better them than me.

Chapter 3

Sly

The God Stripe was hidden behind clouds the night she was born. Whether that's a blessing or a curse depends on who you ask.

—The case of *Moira Vex v. The Council of War*, opening statements

The sun had barely finished setting, but already the barracks was full of laughter, smoke, and the smell of fermented fruit. Once upon a time Templar Malcom's squad had been something to fear. They had trained all day alongside Templar Zorra and Templar Mullen's own recruits. Those days had ended long before Sly had been recruited.

She sat up in her bunk watching Radcliffe and the others shuffle a stack of hexes, preparing to pass their hard-earned credits back and forth to each other into the early hours of the morning. Sly had no problem with gambling or with having friends on the squad, but she was growing restless. When she enlisted, she had pledged herself to Templar Malcolm because of his reputation of being Baron Tamiyo's chosen blade. The stories of lore promised that he was the righteous fist of the Baron. A tool of the God Stripe trusted with the most critical missions. A legendary warrior who wielded rare artifacts that rained fire down on enemies of the Chain. He was meant to be her key to glory. Her path to the God Stripe's secrets and power. Since she'd arrived, she'd found him to be little more than a grumpy, drunk old man. He barely had the drive to show up to training most days.

"Sly, should we deal you in?" Fritz called from across the floor as he randomized the hexes for their next wager.

Radcliffe jumped in before she had a chance to politely decline. "Why do you even ask, Fritz? You know Templar Sly is far too serious for childish games. Isn't that right?"

Radcliffe had a face that was somehow both handsome and painfully punchable at the same time. Luckily Sly had plenty of chances to do just that since the two were frequent sparring partners. On the rare days that Malcolm did show up for training he often paired Sly and Radcliffe up for drills. They were clearly the two strongest recruits in the bunch, and if anyone lived to become a templar, it would be one of the pair. Sly didn't mind the competition. Radcliffe kept her sharp. She got the distinct impression he saw her as a threat though.

"He's right, Fritz. If you want my credits I'm afraid you'll have to fight me for them. I'm not in the habit of just setting them on the table and letting the fates sweep them away." Sly grinned back at the group. It didn't serve her to be seen as an outsider. She needed this lot to believe in her.

Radcliffe stood up and cracked his knuckles. "A fight, huh? What do you say, 50 credits from the first to tap out?"

Elm, who had been busy sharpening a spear in the corner of the room, sat up at the chance to make a few credits. She scratched the shaved side of her head and eyed the pair. "I'll put 50 credits on Sly."

Metz leaned back in his chair at the hexes table and started counting his chips. "I'll take 50 on Cliffe, but if he loses I'll have to drop out of hexes for the night."

Radcliffe slapped his own credits down on the table and began pulling off his shirt. Sly couldn't help but roll her eyes. She sprung off her bunk and pulled out 50 credits from her own stash. "Weapons?"

The door to the barracks swung open and Templar Malcolm's towering shadow fell on the group before Radcliffe could define the terms of the challenge.

"Enough, sproutlings. Get dressed, get sober, get outside. We've been summoned by the Baron." He left the room in stunned silence.

Sly tried to hold back a grin as she grabbed her polearm and stormed out of the barracks. It was finally happening. Her chance had arrived.

Chapter 4

Beth

The rebellion began in the streets. Vandalism, whispers, and just enough of the truth.

—From the journal of Aphra of Alpha, Colonel of the Truthkeepers

It had been dark for little more than an hour, and candlelight was shining bright in Portia's shop as Beth jogged through the slums. Technically curfew started at sundown, but patrols weren't very strict in this corner of the island. The guard units were led by upper-island scum, but most of the foot soldiers doing the actual work and patrolling were low-island born.

Joining the Baron's forces wasn't a great way to make friends on the lower islands, but it paid better and was less dangerous than joining a fishing crew. The patrols were often open to bribes too, which meant they ended up getting paid twice—once from the crown and once from their neighbors to turn a blind eye. For the right kind of person, that payout was worth the lack of real friends.

The bell above the door chimed as Beth entered the shop to find Portia sitting on the counter. Her chin was resting on her hand and she looked to Beth as she carried on her conversation. "Look, friend, if you want to travel up an island and visit your highborn-sally, this is your best bet." Portia said.

The customer went white with fear as he looked from Portia to Beth. "You trying to get me killed before I even set sail in this death trap?"

"Relax. She's not interested in your forbidden affair."

Beth winked at the man in reassurance before wandering off behind the counter to let Portia finish reeling him in. "Secret's safe with me. Who am I to stand in the way of love?"

She's got him right where she wants him.

Beth was in a rush, but she could spare a few minutes to watch Portia work her magic. It wasn't that Portia ripped people off. No, she just had a way of helping them spend more credits than they intended. Portia ran a hand through her springy curls and feigned concern as she listened to the man try to talk himself out of the deal. The mark must've been about ten years older than Beth and Portia, but they had a reputation on Beta. Beth and Portia could find, make, or smuggle just about anything. And it wasn't like anyone lived very long on the lower islands anyway, so dealing with teenagers running businesses, heists, and deals was just part of bottom island life.

"Even if the price wasn't insane, this thing looks like it'll get me killed. I'll be shark food before I get there. And let's say I do make it to Charlie—how do I get surface-side? Does this thing fly too?"

"Come on now, pal. We both know you can't afford the flying model." Portia smiled at the customer as she reached below the counter and pulled out a harness and climbing ropes. "It's a forty-foot climb. Easy stuff for a strong guy like you, no doubt. I'll throw in the climbing gear for an extra twenty credits."

"Oh, great. So if I don't drown, I can fall to my death. To the depths with me either way, right?"

Portia had been closing deals like this since she was old enough to count credits. The store belonged to her auntie back then, but passed down to Portia officially three years ago when Auntie Maya started getting too sick to run the shop. First she couldn't make it through a full shift, but it wasn't long before she couldn't even make it down the ladders from their cramped living space in the stacks to the streets below. Portia took over the store then and it was just a few months later that they sent Auntie Maya out into the water to be judged by the depths. Beth didn't buy into the ceremony much, but if anyone really deserved to fly up to the God Stripe and live forever, it was that one. She held Portia's hand and prayed with her while Auntie sank below the waves and into the afterlife.

"You're welcome to take your chances with the bridges. If you think the boat's expensive, wait until you hear the rates those sentries are charging . . . or you could just let her find a top islander to keep her bed warm, if that's more your speed."

Credits changed hands, and Portia showed the sucker how to break down the collapsible sail. Though small, she was strong, and she had no trouble jamming the whole contraption back in on itself. In its portable form it was no bigger than a backpack. He slung it over his shoulder and left the shop.

"You know they're going to kill him when he gets caught in her bed?" Beth blurted out before the door had even closed.

Portia shrugged. "Like you said, who are we to stand in the way of love?"

"Such a romantic. Hope that wasn't your last boat in stock, by the way. We've got a trip to make."

"We do?" Portia asked.

Before Portia could press for any more details, Beth had ducked below the counter and started pulling out supplies. "Where are your swamp boots?"

"*Swamp boots*? Oh hell no. What kind of crazy lead did Mitch give you?"

Beth placed a few canteens and ration packs on the counter. She shuffled through the drawers for a stash of dried seaweed pouches and added those to the pile, as well. The seaweed was Portia's favorite snack on longer jobs that would keep them away from the usual neighborhood fish fries that took place most evenings on Beta. Once she felt she had enough food for a day or two, Beth climbed a nearby shelf to reach the ceiling.

"No Mitch on this job. Just the two of us."

She's not going to be happy about Mitch's nose. We should probably get off island before he parades over here.

"Come on, Beth. We just made a huge score off that fruit. With this boat and climbing bundle, we're set for this moon."

Beth pushed a tile aside in the ceiling, reached into the opening, and dropped down a few short coral daggers onto her stack of supplies. The shop was officially Portia's, but they'd been running it together - and living out of its back office - since before Auntie Maya passed. It was home.

"Can you at least get your head out of the ceiling and tell me what the job is?" Portia asked.

"It just fell out of the sky. You didn't see it?"

"The striping space rocks?! Have you lost your mind? They'll string us up from the bridges when we get caught."

And that's if they go easy on us.

"We never get caught, Portia. We've made swamp runs before. This is no different. We'll be back on the island before anyone even notices we're gone."

"No different? You know the Baron sends out full squads of templars when God Rocks fall from the sky. Actual templars and recruits with armor and weapons from the heavens. We'll be racing a boat full of soldiers for a score that we don't even understand."

They want it, so it's got to be valuable.

"And we'll win that race. We've got a three-island lead. And I heard you make the fastest illegal sailboats in the Chain."

"That's just what I tell lover boys who want to get themselves killed heading to a noble bed. This is dangerous, B. Even for us."

"But this could change everything. No more shady deals with Mitch. No more working the shop from dawn to well after dark every day. Who knows, maybe we'll find a safe little hideaway on the way over there . . ."

Portia jumped the counter and slid to the opposite side before Beth could do any more smooth talking.

"Beth, don't. A safe little hideaway? You know there's nothing but mud, bugs, and death on the mainland."

She was right. Inland was a death trap. Why else would everyone stay under the Baron's rule if they could leave the islands and live happily ever after? Factions had tried in the past. Some even made it all the way through the swamps, but none had ever made it any farther than that. Death comes quickly on the mainland. Whether it's from the birds, the bugs, or an elite squad of templars, a dry and shallow grave is the only guarantee for fools who venture off the islands.

Beth and Portia were no fools. It was true that they'd made successful swamp runs in the past. The difference this time was that they wouldn't be the only ones on the way to the contraband.

"We'll be back by tomorrow night. You, me, and the greatest score a couple of low-island hustlers have ever dreamed of."

Portia crinkled her nose. Just like she always did before she was about to crack.

"I'm only going along with this 'cause you'll get yourself killed if you go alone. You can't sail to save your life. You know that, right?"

Beth bit her lip and tried not to let her excitement show too much as she slapped Portia's mud boots onto the counter.

"You remember where you stashed our scaling gear after the close call on the Depth Walker dock job though, right?" Portia asked.

The high Beth had been riding since the God Rocks fell out of the sky suddenly disappeared.

"Striping Alpha . . ." Beth muttered.

Portia laughed and moved for the door. "It'll be better to scale down from there anyway, right? And it's getting late. He's probably passed out already. You won't even have to talk to him."

"Yeah. Let's hope." Beth followed Portia to the door with noticeably less enthusiasm than she had entered with.

"Or we could just call it off." Portia suggested.

"No. He's not ruining this. Let's get down there."

Portia flipped the sign in the front window from OPEN to CLOSED. She had no idea it would be the last time.

Chapter 5

Malcolm

A recruit is only as strong as the templar they follow. But a templar . . . a templar swings their sword with all the might of the God Stripe.

—Proverbs of Templar Amaryte

The word *green* wasn't quite enough to capture just how striping fresh this batch of recruits were. In the lot of them, maybe one would live long enough to prove themselves a true templar. Malcolm didn't have the luxury of being picky with his trainees these days, though. Recruitment was down and times were changing. He was a rusty relic in this army and everyone knew it. Before long, the last of all the old templars would be dead or offloaded to noncombat duty like that cowardly bastard, Jonah. Senior Adviser to the Baron . . . if she had seen Jonah's behavior on the front lines with her own eyes like Malcolm had, she might reconsider taking that sage advice of his.

Malcolm sat on a boulder a dozen or so lengths away from his squad. He'd been on Delta a long time, but somehow the Baron's gardens still managed to take his breath away. The open space the top island had on its surface was unlike anything a bottom islander could ever know. He was lucky to be here. He never lost sight of that. He always found a way to take a moment and soak in the green leaves. The fresh scent of the buds blooming.

From a distance, he could easily be mistaken for a younger man thanks to his broad shoulders and hulking form. It was only up close that his scars and wrinkles revealed how many moons he'd already lived through. The aging templar pretended not to hear his squad's banter while he admired some nearby vegetation. He was too old and too tired to keep the sproutlings in line every moment of the day. If at least half of them were alive at the end of this mission, that'd be enough to satisfy his duty.

"You ever met the Baron, Sly? Tamiyo the Cruel? I've heard she's even more gorgeous than the stories claim. And unwed too . . . I might have to make a move."

Radcliffe. Most would find his sharp features and athletic frame attractive if he could keep his mouth shut long enough not to sour them with his underdeveloped sense of wit. Malcolm could ignore a lot of things, but not a direct jest at the Baron.

"And I heard she likes to cut the tongues out of green recruits who don't know when to shut the stripe up." The veteran templar stood up from the boulder and moved closer to the group as they fell silent.

"Templar Malcolm heard right, I'm afraid."

At the sound of her voice the half dozen recruits fell into line, weapons at their sides and eyes straight ahead. Her silk gown was long enough to drag smoothly across the ground behind her as she walked toward the squad. Her feet were covered by the flowing dress and gave the illusion that she was gliding over the rocks and soil. Her long black hair spilled over her exposed shoulders and down her back as her entourage, including Jonah, lingered behind.

"Unfortunately, most of my reliable recruits were lost in a tragic wyvern accident last winter. So rather than feeding your tongue to the fish, Templar . . . ?"

She idled in front of Radcliffe awaiting a response. Her gown may not offer the same protection that their heavy sea scrap forged armor did, but there was no confusion about who was operating from the position of power in this exchange.

"Just Radcliffe, my lady. Not a real templar yet."

But she already knew that, of course. Malcolm smirked at the way she made Radcliffe squirm.

"Well, then, rather than feeding your tongue to the fish, *recruit* Radcliffe, I'll allow you to keep it for your first journey inland."

Tamiyo released Radcliffe from her stare and redirected her gaze toward the skies over the mainland. Everyone followed her line of sight except for Malcolm, who kept his eyes on her.

"Hunt down the God Rock, bring me its gifts, and the best among you will be templars when you return. Templar Malcolm can tell you how imperative it is that you do not fail. The survival of our entire community, from bottom island beggar to Charlie Lord, and all the way up to me, will suffer the consequences if you falter."

Malcolm opened his mouth for the first time since she appeared. "We're ready to sail out immediately, Baron."

Tamiyo shrugged while giving the retrieval team the first hint of a smile. "Well then. Don't let me hold you back, soldiers. Stripe off already."

A hint of amusement cracked through on the face of every

recruit. Even Radcliffe, whose cheeks were still red from the verbal lashing. She'd managed to win them over with one curse. Malcolm tried to remember if that's how she'd gained his undying loyalty all those years ago. Back when he was already a grown man and she was still a child. He'd been willing to charge into water cyclones or devil birds at that girl's command for as long as she had allowed him to. And he had the scars to prove it.

As the recruits began to gather their gear and head off to the lift, Tamiyo raised a finger that said, "Just one more thing."

"Templar Malcolm?"

The smile faded from her face once she stood close enough to be shielded from sight behind his frame.

"Yes, my lady?"

"Let's try to bring someone besides yourself back in one piece this time, yeah? Just for a change of pace. For old time's sake."

She was already striding back to her tower at the Citadel before the weathered templar could muster a response. Her lapdog Jonah trailed along at her heels without ever meeting eyes with Malcolm.

Moments after she was gone, Malcolm muttered, "You have my word, Tamiyo."

Chapter 6

Beth

Not everyone was willing to destroy history. Siblings fought against siblings. And parents against parents.

—From the journal of Aphra of Alpha, Colonel of the Truthkeepers

Life on Beta was brutal. There was no denying the oppression of living on the lower islands. Days were spent at grueling jobs that paid close to nothing and all of the output went back up to Charlie and Delta for the royalty to redistribute however they saw fit. Nights were spent dodging curfew patrols and trying to make any extra bit of credits that could actually keep you fed. But still, Beth knew things could be even worse. She'd spent her first thirteen years on Alpha.

If Beta was overcrowded then Alpha was downright claustrophobic. The stacks were uneven and poorly made. The sea bones towered up to the skies anyway and not a year went by without a tragedy bringing a whole neighborhood crashing to the ground. If anyone survived those accidents, they'd usually wish they hadn't.

Beth was born a bottom islander. She spent her earliest years with her parents. She didn't know any other life back then. She didn't know to be angry or jealous. Her mother had a baby when Beth was six and a half and suddenly she was a sister. For a small window of time, it was the four of them. Walking through the slums of Alpha now, heading to her Dad's place, she tried to recall anything about that sibling. She remembered her crying at night from hunger. The noise didn't bother Beth, but the neighbors in the stack above them pounded on the floor, screaming at her parents to shut the striping demon up before someone tossed it into the depths. Beth's dad stormed out of their stack after the outburst and came back not five minutes later with a satisfied look on his face and his hand wrapped in a rag. As far as Beth could remember, she never heard a sound from the stack above theirs again.

Beth squeezed through a tight alley and reached for the familiar ladder leading up to her father's stack. This wasn't the same one from all those years ago. He lived on his own now in a smaller model. She tried to stay off of Alpha unless a job brought her down the Chain. She and her father weren't close these days.

After climbing high enough that she could feel the winds clawing at her she hopped off the ladder and slid through the unlocked entrance to Stack 14K. The numerals counted the level up and the letter was the name for the full column. Her dad's column, affectionately known as Killtown on Alpha, wasn't somewhere you'd want to linger around. Leaving a door unlocked in Killtown may seem like asking for trouble, but Beth's father had a reputation and the local gangs knew better than to test the old man.

Beth made for the closet just inside the entryway and quietly shifted her father's cloaks to the side to uncover the climbing gear. She slung her backpack off and let it rest on the ground while she took a quick inventory.

"I was waiting for you last full moon. Thought you might show up this year."

Stripe. Couldn't be lucky enough to find him passed out.

"The shop's been busy, you know how work can be. Just needed to pick some stuff up. I'll be out of your hair in a minute." Beth said.

Her father leaned back against the far wall. He was trying to keep himself in the shadows, but Beth could see the redness in his eyes. He was drowning in self pity and memories, and she wasn't about to let him drag her to the depths as he sunk. She'd done her time here. Those years with just the two of them. She tried so striping hard to help lift him up, but she'd never be enough. She knew that now.

"It was your sister's birthday, Beth. You should've been here. You owe her that." His voice broke, but he pushed through. He wasn't going to stop until she was feeling as guilty as he was to be alive. "You owe your mom that."

Beth slid the climbing gear into her backpack and turned away from her father. She stopped as her hand gripped the windowsill, but didn't turn back.

"I don't have a sister, Dad. Or a mom. And you don't have a wife."

She didn't mean to be cruel. She just refused to live in the past the way he did. Anniversaries and birthday parties for ghosts.

"Watch your mouth, Beth. Those highborn bastards took almost everything from us. They can't take my memories. And you shouldn't let them take yours either."

"You only have one daughter left. And I'm not going to sit

around and cry while I wait for whatever scraps Delta decides to pass down the Chain to us."

Beth lept to the ladder and started her climb down. Curfew was coming and she was ready to dive off the side of the Chain if that's what it would take to get her mind off of the past.

CHAPTER 7

JONAH

The Baron is chosen, but the burden can't be carried alone. The weight of the God Stripe demands more strength than a single soul can provide.

—Excerpt from the departure letter of Lord Drolt, Senior Adviser to Baron Agrius

The rules about what to do when a God Rock came crashing down were incredibly clear to all those who had a role to play in the recovery. First, the geographers were to track the path and determine a rough estimate of where the point of impact would be. This step, although it may sound incredibly difficult, always went off without a hint of trouble . . . except this time.

Although gifts from the heavens are unpredictable, and sometimes years can pass without any miracles falling from the sky, the advisers and handmaidens had ensured that a pair of geographers was always in the watchtower monitoring the skies. The watchtower itself sat on Charlie, the third island, and was the only structure in the Chain that stood as tall as the Baron's own chambers. It was operated by two trained geographers at any given time. The pair worked together in shifts and were relieved of duty every other sunrise. It was a system with multiple redundancies built in that had operated flawlessly for decades.

When Jonah rushed across the bridge to Charlie and stormed up the stairs of the watchtower after seeing this particular God Rock fall—the first since he had taken on the role of Senior Adviser to the Baron—he found the geographers in a bit of a compromising position.

Jonah assumed that mere minutes after a God Rock had fallen the duo would be pouring over maps and scouting reports and putting the finishing touches on their recommendation to pass on to the retrieval team. Rather than that, it appeared that Lucius and Talia had decided to take in a romantic evening and were enjoying each other's company just a tad more so than geographer pairs were intended to do.

Once again, Jonah had found himself in an impossible situation that was spiraling out of his control. Sending the young lovebirds out the top window of the watchtower certainly crossed his mind, but that would only expose the mistake. He hadn't hand-selected the geographers and assigned their shifts, but this sort of blunder had a way of taking everyone down with it once it reached the Baron's ear. She hadn't earned the name Tamiyo the Cruel without good cause.

So, he made a decision. That's why she gave him this position after all, right? His ability to think on his feet and adjust to the unexpected twists that could arrive on the battlefield, in the courts, or on the streets. He was a fixer. And he would find a way to fix this. First off, by containing the situation.

After putting the fear of the God Stripe, the depths, and

everything in between into Lucius and Talia, Jonah calmly walked them to the observatory looking glass and instructed them to draw up their recommendation. Immediately.

Smoke still rose from the landing site, which was a blessing for the geographers, who otherwise would've been working entirely in the dark. If the God Rock had landed in the water, there would be no recovery from this sort of error. Jonah counted his blessings from above and below.

The geographers did the best they could based on where the smoke was rising and Jonah's recounting of the fall. The angle of the fall, the speed, the color of the tail. So many striping questions. Lucius brought up verifying Jonah's account with a second source before finalizing their recommended search location, but the look in the retired templar's eyes quickly shut down that course of action. Nobody would ever learn what happened there that evening. The pair of geographers were taking turns watching the skies, as they should have been, and managed to perfectly record every detail about the descent and landing. By the books. Their records should indicate as much when he returned for the unabridged report in the morning. For now, he would take the immediate recommendation and pass it on to the Baron. There was nothing to be concerned about because they had done everything exactly as they were trained.

Jonah knew he would eventually have to tie up these loose ends, but it would be far too suspicious to do so anytime soon. After the retrieval party was back, he would handle the geographers. There had to be consequences, but there was no point in bothering the Baron with those sorts of details.

Chapter 8

Beth

Blood flowed through the stacks of the low islands, but it was too late. The truth had already emerged.

—From the journal of Aphra of Alpha, Colonel of the Truthkeepers

"Bird droppings." Portia muttered as Beth reached down to help pull her up to the next rooftop. This was the fastest way to get around Alpha after curfew. After the detour to her father's stack, Beth knew they had to make good time to stay ahead of whatever force the Baron would be sending out after the treasure. Guards patrolled the rocky streets below, but most shifts turned a blind eye to anything happening over their heads on top of the makeshift housing structures. The uneven rooftops made for a safer path to just about any corner of the overcrowded island . . . as long as you weren't afraid of heights.

"When did you turn into such a skeptic? You've seen firsthand how much profit there is in debris." Getting Portia to come along was one thing, but convincing her the trip was a good idea? That might not happen until payment was in hand and they had both walked away from the job with all of their limbs still attached.

They jumped from rooftop to rooftop together. The gusts of powerful wind high above the choppy waters could send an inexperienced jumper plummeting to their death, but Beth and Portia were far from inexperienced. They'd been making these sort of late-night runs since they were kids, sneaking off to find some privacy away from their respective crews. Portia's childhood stack was overflowing with neighbors who were close enough to call siblings, aunts, and uncles; Beth's was teeming with herb-runners, hired muscle, and even the occasional corrupt Charlie highborn making the trip down a few islands to arrange some scheme or another. Either way, there wasn't a lot of quiet time for the pair in their respective homes.

"All you see is credit signs. I'm trying to be the smart one here. I'm talking about *prospect theory*. There's way more to lose than there is to gain when we make a play like this . . ."

Portia put her economics lesson on hold and held up a finger to point out a guard rounding the corner on patrol below. It was likely the guard would ignore them even if they were spotted, but it was best not to push their luck.

The guard's footsteps echoed away into the distance, and Portia carried on as they leaped to the next stack. "This treasure hunter game is bad for business and, more importantly, bad for our life expectancy."

The pair reached the edge of the housing structures and looked down over a rocky cliff face leading to the waters below. The trunk of the island was a few hundred lengths tall, which made the surface of the water a long way down. Not an impossible obstacle with the right climbing gear, but definitely enough of a drop to keep the average citizen fully locked into their island when the bridges and lifts were closed.

"Doesn't the fact that you wouldn't know words like *prospect theory* and *life expectancy* without the tomes we found while treasure hunting cancel out your argument? Forget about the money. They're hiding *knowledge*. I know that's enough to piss you off."

Portia laughed off Beth's retort as they started digging through their packs and pulling out the necessary climbing gear.

"Don't even play like stealing a rotting box of contraband books is the same as going off-island to hunt down a God Rock."

Beth feigned offense at the rebuttal. "Well, not exactly the same . . . but in the same realm of heresy for sure. Almost definitely."

Laws had never been Beth's strong suit.

They found a suitable spot to begin their descent, and Beth attached one anchor to a nearby ledge while Portia did the same with another. Two-point equalized anchors were the safest way to repel down the cliff side when the official lifts to the port were being heavily guarded.

"Or is it treason? I can never remember the difference . . ." Beth was mostly musing to herself at this point as she prepared for the descent.

She stepped up to the edge and leaned backward while Portia shook her head.

"You better jump off this cliff before I throw you off it." Portia smiled and waved as Beth disappeared over the ledge. She began double- and triple-checking the anchor points as the rope slowly fed through.

"Or is it anarchy? Laws are kind of confusing," Beth asked as she found her footing on the side of the island's trunk.

Portia whispered back over the side of the ledge, "Are you still talking?"

She took a knee and leaned out over the edge to meet eyes with Beth, who was only a few feet below her. She was concentrating too hard on what was in front of her to notice the shadows sneaking up on the rooftop behind her.

"Think I coulda been a judge if I was born a few islands up?" Beth asked as she looked up.

"Ignoring you forever," Portia whispered in defeat as Beth started to let go of the slack and slowly scale her way down the island trunk.

Portia had a brief moment to look out over the sea and imagine what they would find when they reached the God Rock before she was interrupted. She should've heard the bootfalls coming far earlier. She had let herself get carried away with excitement and became distracted. Now that they were close, she knew the owner just from the sound. This was the first time she'd let someone as heavy-footed as Mitch get the jump on her since she could tie her own laces.

"Had a feeling you might be making a run for the rock," Portia said with a casual smile as she turned to face Mitch. He and two of his pals were standing on the rooftop of the sea bones one level up from Portia. Each of Mitch's henchmen had a dagger raised over one of the two anchors that were holding Beth's support rig in place. The color drained from Portia's face as she realized Beth had crossed him one too many times. A fragile man like Mitch can only take so much embarrassment before he snaps.

"I'm not here to race you to the rock, Portia. I'm done with your trash." Mitch jumped down to her level and stood between Portia and his goons.

"I'm here to send you both to the depths... And take your store as payment for all the times you've burned me."

Chapter 9

Malcolm

A templar's blade and shield are nothing without a reliable squad to ride into battle with.

—Proverbs of Templar Amaryte

The retrieval crew was sailing away from Delta as quickly as their small vessel would allow. The boat was big enough to hold the team of five recruits plus Malcolm with just a bit of spare deck space to stretch their legs. It would only take about half a day to reach the inland swamps if the wind kept up at the current pace and the team was in good spirits. Any nerves about what awaited on solid land were at least temporarily washed away by Tamiyo's inspiring words. For everyone except Malcolm, that was.

"So I told the third-island trash, I'll be taking the food *and* the whore, and I won't be paying for either."

Striping Radcliffe. The fool doesn't realize how close he just came to actually losing his tongue to the Baron, and already he's running his mouth again.

Malcom's patience for the lad was fading rapidly.

Surely Tamiyo wouldn't mind if that one didn't make it back, right?

"Well I hope you got your rocks off while you could, Cliffe. 'Cause where we're heading there aren't any low-island tramps to impress with your fantasy stories." Sly interrupted Radcliffe's impromptu comedy routine with a smirk, but her frequent sparring partner was clearly not entertained by the contradiction to his bravado.

Malcolm took a swig from something too strong to share with his recruits as the tension built and all eyes turned to Radcliffe to see how he would respond. Malcolm had been watching these two train for long enough to know Sly's wiry frame and small stature shouldn't be underestimated. The dark-haired girl's skin somehow always seemed to be red, as if she'd never adjusted to life under the sun.

"Fantasy? Are you implying I'm a liar, Sly? I suppose you would recognize one of your own, wouldn't you?"

She didn't bite. Malcolm wasn't sure what Radcliffe was implying with the accusation, nor did he really care.

"I'm suggesting you haven't used that sword for anything more than trying to impress Beta hags who pretend to be buying your stories and then still find a way to charge you after your thirty seconds are up."

Radcliffe's face turned from golden tan to sunset red, though still a shade less blushed than Sly's permanent burn, and his hand wandered toward the weapon at his side.

"This is a brand new sword, actually. The last one broke over someone's skull. Let's see if this one holds up any better . . ."

Malcolm's interest piqued as the rivalry turned from verbal jabs to actual blows. Despite the disciplinary fallout, this sort of bout was common among groups of recruits. Especially when there were multiple alphas vying for the top spot.

Sly hadn't seemed the pack leader type when she first arrived, but her speed and strength skyrocketed her to the front of the squad whether she wanted to be there or not. The fact that she could mentally run circles around poor Cliffe didn't help much either. It wasn't just strength that mattered in a battle. Wits like hers are what could keep a squad alive when plans fall the stripe apart.

"This oughta be striping entertaining." Malcolm chuckled to himself as he pocketed his bottle and turned to watch.

Sly didn't waste any time drawing a weapon of her own as Radcliffe looked down to his belt at a snail's pace in comparison. She equipped the polearm off her back as smoothly as a bird glides over the water.

"Get her, Cliffe!" The other recruits quickly took sides and backed up to make space for the spat on the tiny deck.

Before Radcliffe had even fully unsheathed his weapon, Sly kicked his hand, forcing the sword back into its sheath. She jabbed Radcliffe in the gut with the blunt end of her polearm and sent him stumbling back toward the railing. Other recruits jumped out of the way as Sly charged forward, now pushing Radcliffe off balance by grasping his shirt with one hand and using the other to hold the polearm to his neck.

He never stood a chance against this one.

Cliffe was leaning backward off the edge of the boat, and Sly held him on board. Their faces were close as she whispered to him, "Be careful spreading rumors, Cliffe. Some lies have consequences."

Malcolm raised his hand and stepped toward his crew.

"Enough, Sly. I think he gets the point."

Radcliffe dropped to the deck as Sly immediately released him at Malcolm's command. She wasn't afraid to break the rules, but she still wouldn't disobey a clear order from a templar of the Baron's inner circle.

Sly extended an open hand towards Radcliffe. "I'll take that 50 credits now."

"Sly may be a pain in the ass, but she's right about one thing... there are no whores where we're heading."

Malcolm took another step forward, approaching the group. Everyone stood at a casual attention, except for Radcliffe, who was still on the ground, processing just how he could have been beaten so soundly when he was the one who started the striping fight.

"I've promised to bring every one of you green bastards back alive from this mission."

Malcolm stopped in front of Radcliffe and knelt down, so the two were eye to eye.

"But boy—"

Radcliffe looked up and faced his commanding officer. The red drained from his cheeks, his skin returned to its usual clear tan complexion, and any embarrassment was replaced with shame.

"Templar?"

Malcolm looked over Radcliffe's head and gazed off toward the coast in the distance.

"You're going to have to be a hell of a lot faster if I'm to deliver on that promise."

Chapter 10

Beth

The lies went higher than anyone could have imagined.

—From the journal of Aphra of Alpha, Colonel of the Truthkeepers

Portia wasn't surprised Beth had pissed off Mitch, but she'd never seen him quite this far over the edge. At least not with his rage pointing in their direction. They'd grown up together. They may not be best friends, but islanders from the same stack looked out for each other. At the very least they didn't hurl each other off the side of any cliffs.

"You can't just kill us, Mitch. We've been working together since we were kids. Just slow down and we'll work something out."

Mitch took a knee and looked Portia in the eyes. He shook his head and let out a chuckle.

"You're right, we have. And you know what?" Mitch

nodded to the goon on his left. "That crazy partner of yours has been ripping me off since we were kids too."

The goon on the left dropped his dagger down and cut through the rope. One anchor down. If the other line were to be cut, there'd be no way Beth could survive the fall.

"No! Are you striping crazy?!" Portia spun around and looked over the side of the cliff. She was fast enough to see the balance point shift and Beth lose her footing.

"What the—" Beth tried to keep a hushed tone, but Portia could hear the panic in her voice as she struggled to keep her balance. "We got a problem up there?"

Mitch grabbed Portia's shoulder and spun her back around. He didn't speak loudly enough for Beth to hear them down below. "The way I see it, the whole Chain is about to have one less problem."

Mitch turned to the goon on his right, preparing to give the signal to send Beth soaring toward the crashing waves below.

"Wait! I've got a better deal for you. Hear me out!" Portia pleaded.

The goon started to bring his blade down over the rope, but Mitch called him off. "Hold on, now. I'm a practical businessman. Let's hear what she has to offer."

Portia breathed the tiniest sigh of relief. She wasn't out of the mess yet, and she was going to have to give up a whole lot more before she would be. "You remember when the templars and recruits raided our stacks? Summer of the drought?"

A whistle from below made Portia turn her head and peer down in the middle of her story. That pitch indicated Beth thought Portia might be in trouble with some patrols. To anyone else it might have just sounded like some seabirds chirping as they flew by below.

"They couldn't grow anything on the upper islands, so

they came down to recall the rations and take anything we had managed to save," Portia continued.

Down below, Beth started to lose her cool. Thirty seconds and no whistle back. Something had gone sideways. Getting busted past curfew wasn't the end of the world. Basically just a slap on the wrist depending on which patrols were out. But the climbing gear, the anchors . . . there'd be no hiding what was going on. And not even the most crooked guards would overlook someone sneaking off the island in the middle of a full lockdown.

Mitch shook his head as he reflected on the memory. "My mom tried hiding some food so I wouldn't starve. We were just kids. What, like eight, nine years old?"

Portia slowly reached for a side pocket on her bag and pulled out something to write on. She started scribbling away. "We were eight. I remember. We heard the screams from three stacks up when they took her."

She continued working on a rudimentary map, and Mitch's face softened just a touch.

"I wouldn't have lived through the summer if you didn't share your secret stash with me," Mitch admitted.

Portia ripped the page she'd been working on out of her notebook and held it out toward Mitch. "There's more than just rations in it now. That's everything I have saved up. Way more than she owed you."

Mitch read over the notes and shook his head. "She's trouble, Portia. Even by our standards. She's been dragging you down for as long as I can remember."

Down below Beth struggled to climb back up. There weren't many grips in the trunk, but she was making slow progress. She wouldn't let them take Portia without a fight.

Mitch took a minute to think on the offer, but he already knew how this was going to play out. "You let us send her to the depths, and you can keep the store. You'll be better off without her. We can even keep working together . . . But if you leave with her to chase down that rock, you can't come back. Beta is my island now. And there's no place for her on it."

Beth mumbled to herself as she furiously climbed, "Don't be dead up there or I'll kick your ass."

Portia slung her bag back over her shoulder and approached the rope that was still anchored to the wall. Her only way down at this point.

"Your auntie put a lot of work into that store—into our whole neighborhood. Is that sea scrap chaser really worth throwing all of it away for?" Mitch asked.

Portia gripped the rope and started to slide over the edge.

"She's the only family I have left, Mitch. Enjoy the loot . . . and your island."

Chapter 11

Sly

I taught her the names of the stars. And which ones would protect her when she needed them.

—The case of *Moira Vex v. The Council of War*, opening statements

Sly couldn't make her brain slow down. She sat up an hour into her restless sleep shift and tapped Fritz on the shoulder.

"Get some extra rest, Fritz. I can take over oars until sunbreak."

"You sure, Sly? I already had my sleep shift." Fritz was a good lad. None of the ego that Radcliffe was always tripping over. Unfortunately he didn't have much confidence either. Sly wasn't so sure he'd be able to hack it once the mainland started trying to tear them apart. He would need the rest more than her.

"I can't sleep. One of us might as well get some shut eye."

Fritz nodded in agreement and switched places with Sly. She took over the oar and looked out at the light of the God Stripe. The reflection spread out across the water drawing a straight line to the shore. Sly imagined feeling the solid ground beneath her boots. Kneeling down and finding grass between her fingers. She was lost in her mainland daydream when Malcolm took a knee next to her.

"The God Stripe guides us to shore tonight, I see." He kept his eyes pointed forward as he addressed her.

Sly snapped out of her daydream and tried to find the words that her commanding officer might want to hear. "A good omen, isn't it, Templar?"

Malcolm chuckled. "I don't put much stock in omens, recruit. I've lost some of my best friends on missions that began with good omens. Good omens or bad, we have our mission."

"Understood, Templar. We have our mission." Sly stole a glance at Templar Malcolm out of the corner of her eye before focusing back on the open water ahead of them.

"What about you, Sly? Who controls your fate? The omens or your own will?" Malcolm looked to the recruit this time. Sly could feel his gaze burning into her, as if he was trying to read her mind. She internally cursed Radcliffe for that jab about her being a liar.

"I follow you, Templar Malcolm. Your orders and the Oaths guide me." She resisted the urge to look up at the stars or out into the mainland, where her heart was still focused.

"You follow me. I follow the Baron. And the Baron follows the God Stripe." He clapped her on the back in approval. "The way it's meant to be, Sly."

Malcolm stood up and walked to the bow. Now that his eyes weren't on her, Sly allowed her focus to lock in on the mainland. They were so close that she couldn't help but smile. She'd been holding it in since they set sail. "Yes, Templar. The way it's meant to be."

"We may just make a templar out of you before this is over."

Sly's grin widened. "If the God Stripe wills it, Templar. And if *you* will it."

Malcolm turned around and grinned back at his top recruit. "It's yours to lose, Sly."

Chapter 12

Beth

When they came for the Truthkeepers on Alpha, the rebels were armed with more than just their new knowledge.

—From the journal of Aphra of Alpha, Colonel of the Truthkeepers

"His island now? Who the stripe does he think he is? The moron can barely pull off a simple Charlie corridor pickpocket. Now he's claiming to be the kingpin of a whole island?" Beth muttered under her breath.

Once Beth and Portia had sailed away from the islands, the immediate danger started to diminish, and anger was taking over. Not getting arrested for heresy on the way off the island was the first obstacle, next they just needed to survive the trip to the crash site.

She went on, "You know we'll figure it out, right? Obviously he's not going to keep everything we've saved over the years. Or your store. Not a chance in the depths. Who does he think he is threatening us like that? We're supposed to be friends. Or at least associates, ya know?"

"His nose looked a little swollen. Think any of his *friends* had something to do with that?" Portia asked.

Portia was right, as always. Beth couldn't exactly act like he'd broken a sacred oath after the beating she gave him. She had left him his payment, though . . . not the payment he wanted, but still. They were even by her account.

"Fair. But he pointed that spear at me first. So the broken nose is his own fault. He's lucky that's the only damage he took," Beth snapped back.

The waters were as calm as they were dark, but the islands were close enough to the mainland that the draw of the tide would carry their vessel to the coastline within just a few hours with the help of some rowing. There were a few guardtowers and lookouts scattered about between the islands and the mainland, but Beth and Portia knew how to dodge those. There shouldn't have been any real danger until they hit the marsh. Assuming they stayed out of the water, that is.

"A broken nose does not equal a free pass to everything we own. That's all I'm saying," Beth continued.

"He was going to kill you, Beth. What'd you want me to do? Throw him over the edge? We weren't killers the last time I checked. We're supposed to be nonviolent smugglers, as a matter of fact. Maybe stop punching our *associates* and we'll—"

Beth held up a finger to signal Portia to quiet down, but she'd already cut herself off. She clocked the patrol boat in the distance just as early as Beth did. It was small, likely only controlled by a single Depth Walker, but it was way off the usual track. Even if it was an off-schedule shift change at one of the watch posts, there was no reason for a boat to be on their course. For the first time, Beth realized just how seriously the Honor Guard was taking this lockdown. Boat patrols surrounding the islands? Those usually only happened when someone was being hunted down.

It was possible Mitch had gone to the patrols and reported Beth and Portia's plan, but that seemed unlikely. Even if he hoped they were dead, Mitch wasn't the type to ever cooperate with royalty. He may not have wanted Beth and Portia to have any luck finding the God Rock, but he would definitely get a chuckle out of the royal retrieval team coming up empty handed.

"Just stay low. He'll pass," Beth whispered. And hoped.

"What if it's not the only boat? What the stripe are they doing out here?" Portia asked.

If she was being honest with herself, Beth would admit she had no idea. There were rumors Baron Tamiyo was growing more strict and cruel as she aged into adulthood, so perhaps she was tightening up security around the lower islands. The understanding had always been that leaving the islands was a death sentence. It was strictly forbidden, but heading into the waters was so dangerous that there wasn't much point in guarding them. Just about everyone who wasn't a templar or Depth Walker that entered the sea had either drowned, been eaten by a beast, or made it inland just in time to get torn apart by something worse in the marshes.

Island life may be grueling and short, but at least most people died of natural causes up there.

The boat faded off into the distance, and the pair relaxed just enough to get moving again.

"Just keep your eyes out and signal if you see anything. I'm sure that's the last of them." Beth barely had the words out before another boat's candlelit deck appeared in their path. The scouting ship was the same size as the last and seemed to be following a similar course.

"They're guarding a perimeter . . . We're striping trapped," Portia whispered.

Beth hated to admit it, but Portia was right.

Chapter 13

Jonah

The Chain is our legacy, and the Baron must protect it at all costs.

—Excerpt from the departure letter of Lord Drolt, Senior Adviser to Baron Agrius

"The God Rock? Everyone is talking about it, but nothing out of the ordinary. Why?"

"I ask the questions here, bottom feeder. Unless you're the one paying for answers now?" Jonah snapped back.

Miles turned away from Jonah as he rolled his blue eyes at the response. He'd been an informant for enough high-island snobs to know how sensitive they could be. Though this was the first time he'd been so close to true royalty. This dusty old templar actually met face to face with the Baron herself on a daily basis. That meant credits. He wasn't going to blow this. He swallowed his pride, straightened his well-worn robes, and tried to get back in Jonah's good graces.

"Sorry, Templar." Miles started to explain, but Jonah quickly cut him off.

"'Sir' will do. I'm the Senior Adviser to the Baron and my templar days are behind me. Continue."

"Right. Sorry, sir. The God Rock . . . business slowed down on Beta when it fell. Everyone saw it come down. The patrols moved the whole island into lockdown before the buzz had even faded. Just . . . the usual, ya know?" Miles said.

"Any chatter about unauthorized retrieval crews leaving from the lower islands?" Jonah probed.

"Depths no. Island hopping is dangerous enough on a normal night, let alone during a lockdown. All the smart operators shut down any jobs they were planning to run this evening and are laying low. They know you'll all be on high alert until you do . . . whatever it is you do when those things fall." Miles looked down at the floor.

In the years since he retired his Sword of Power, Jonah had done the legwork to establish a reliable network of snitches and informants willing to keep him apprised about any shady deals happening between Alpha and Delta. He'd pulled in every one of his sources he could get to that night. Although security was tripled during a retrieval lockdown, the scum knew the Honor Guard would be . . . distracted. If Jonah were someone who wanted to strike against the throne, which obviously he would never do, he always felt during a retrieval would be the perfect time to act.

According to every one of his low-island associates, nothing of the sort was in the works. Aside from some reports about a handful of rival thieves getting into a spat on Beta, the night was virtually clear of criminal activity.

Jonah tossed a small pouch full of credits to Miles and waved him away. It was enough to make the snitch value their arrangement, but small enough to keep him hungry. To keep him coming back for more.

"Send for an escort back if you hear anything else. I need you back in the stacks. Can't risk you missing something now."

Miles knew the routine. He exited through a door hidden inside Jonah's wardrobe. Second-island street scum couldn't exactly roam through the halls of the royal estate. He'd be met by a guard at the bottom of the passageway and discreetly transported back across the bridge to his own island during the next watch rotation. As long as Miles kept his head down and his hood up, nobody would be the wiser that he'd ever set foot on sacred ground.

The privilege of being invited to Delta was reserved for very few who weren't born into royalty. The Baron's immediate advisers, the Heir and her handmaidens, the Honor Guard, and the most skilled gardeners on the Chain were the only citizens who actually lived on Delta. It was by far the least populated island in the Chain, and for good reason. Protecting the most elite members of the ruling class was the obvious reason for the strict security surrounding Delta visits, but even that was mostly misdirection.

The real treasures to protect on Delta weren't people at all, they were plants. Although some very skilled heretics on Beta could get a bean plant to sprout if they managed to steal or smuggle the seeds, there was next to no living vegetation on the lowest two islands. Charlie had vegetable gardens that provided the produce for all the whole population of the Chain. Those precious fruits and vegetables were the most valuable and rare resource in the Chain's economy. At least as far as the public knew.

Behind the high walls beyond the Delta bridge were luscious gardens full of vegetables and herbs the lower-islanders had never even heard of, let alone tasted. The lack of inhabitants on Delta allowed for expanded growing spaces, and the island's height, which towered over the others in the

Chain, kept it bathed in sunlight throughout the year. The island's walls only faced the other islands, leaving the ocean facing side of the pillar fully exposed to the light from above. This was a calculated risk considering the damage that water cyclones could do to the royal island from the exposed side, but the benefits of the harvest far outweighed any lives lost to the occasional strong wind.

The greatest risk to bringing his low-island spies to his own quarters, rather than meeting them on Charlie, was the possibility this secret could make its way to the common people. Although Delta was impenetrable from the outside thanks to its higher grounds and well-equipped forces, the threat of a revolution was the last thing the Baron needed to deal with. Charging Delta in an attempt to overthrow the throne offered the people nothing but bloodshed. Even if they did succeed, what would they gain? Just a big tower and some fancy clothes, as far as they knew. But if the people knew the island was full of food? That would be a different story . . . And that's not even to mention the artifacts buried deep below the tower.

But Jonah was safe. And he never left loose ends hanging longer than necessary. His escorts kept a short leash on the informants during their commutes, and they never went anywhere near the gardens or food stores. Even if they weren't being forcefully shuttled around with spears in their backs, they shouldn't ever have the opportunity to spot anything that would give away the secrets of Delta's resources.

Would Tamiyo the Cruel approve of his visitors? The council of other advisers and the Heir's handmaidens certainly would not But Jonah liked to think Tamiyo approved of any job done well. She didn't need to be bogged down in the details of exactly how he learned what was going on throughout the Chain or who tipped him off about heresy throughout the islands. She wanted his advice; that's what he was there for. That was his job. As far as the blasphemy of allowing low islanders to set foot on the holy Delta ground . . . he honestly thought it bothered him more than it would the Baron. For all her seriousness, Tamiyo had never seemed the religious type to him. It was a strange quality for a Baron, whose sole purpose was to enforce the will of the God Stripe onto the people.

Tamiyo's predecessor had appeared deeply religious in every encounter Jonah ever had with the man. He frequently visited Charlie to pray with the masses and was known for his extravagant festivities during each annual Stripe Passing. He had extended the typical two sun ceremony to a weeklong event including parties that raged from Delta all the way down to the slums of Alpha. At the end of the festivities, Baron Agrius would lead the Honor Guard in lighting dozens of torches to release out into the sea, to light the way up from the depths. After a person's life had ended, they were sent to the depths below for judgment. Those whose souls were deemed worthy were then said to follow the light of the stars and moons and ascend to the God Stripe. Baron Agrius sent out the candles as a little extra help for those souls who couldn't see quite clearly enough to find their way back up.

It didn't take long for the rest of the Chain to catch on to the former Baron's new tradition, and within just a few years, the end to every Stripe Passing was marked by thousands of torches falling to the sea or being pushed out on makeshift rafts from sea scraps. For one day a year only, the guards turned a blind eye to rules that prohibited the lower islanders from handling fire outside of their hearths or making the trip down to the surface.

Jonah had grown to enjoy the tradition, even if he didn't necessarily believe in it. A spirit either knew its way to the God Stripe or it didn't. No amount of candlelight on the surface could raise a spirit from the depths if it had failed its judgment. There were no second chances.

Tamiyo had wasted no time reverting to the traditional Stripe Passing length when her rule began. Apparently, two days of praise was more than enough for the young Baron.

She wasn't anti-religious or even anti-Agrius. Not that Jonah had seen in his years of service, at least. From the best he could understand, she wanted to signal the beginning of a new era. Baron Agrius had ascended. The age of Baron Tamiyo had begun.

CHAPTER 14

BETH

Life beyond the Chain was a gamble, but the world was growing.

—From the journal of Aphra of Alpha, Colonel of the Truthkeepers

The sun had been down for about three turns, and Dom should've been reading the latest adventures of *Baron Prime and The First Templars*, but instead he was circling Alpha on a one-walker boat until the sun came up. When you're a young man, the Royal Guards come to your island and explain why you should join the Honorbound Order of Templars, the Depth Walkers, or The Skybound; they sell each branch of the Royal service on its potential for glory.

Dom had seen through the propaganda from the very beginning. He was lucky to be born on Charlie, he knew that much, but his family's wealth was quickly deteriorating. If he wanted to stay well fed and help keep his siblings housed on

Charlie, then he had no choice but to survive. He was the oldest of the pack and, although they were tough kids, he knew how Betas treated upper-island families who got pushed out. Moving down an island may not be a direct death sentence, but it was certainly little more than a delayed one.

Although it had the scariest name, Dom saw the Depth Walkers for what it was—an easy ride. Learn to sail, go fishing every day, and skim the water for sea bones. He never understood why more people didn't sign up. For most kids, it probably boiled down to a fear of the depths. Dom had been out on these waters more than most, though, and he'd looked into the swirling pools and waves. He'd never seen the face of a water demon. Not even during his first year when he went overboard during a training session and felt the tides pull him farther and farther from his vessel. No demons clawing at his heels and no trapped spirits pulling him down to join them. Just cold, dark nothing. Scary in its own way, but nothing to keep him from rising to the surface and climbing back aboard, save his own fatigue.

On the night of the falling, he was supposed to be off duty, though. Apparently the God Stripe had other plans for him. So, there he was. Riding in circles around an island and looking for . . . anything. His orders were as vague as they were frustrating. "Circle Alpha and keep an eye out for anything out of the ordinary. If you spot something, report back to the Beta checkpoint immediately. Otherwise, stay on rotation until relief arrives."

Until relief arrives at dawn? The next day? The next week? Anything out of the usual like Depth monsters? Runaways? Smugglers? But Dom had learned not to question these things outside of his own mind. He would put in his shift, and then he'd be back in his bunk with his books soon enough. Maybe even with some overtime credits lining his pockets. Serving as a Depth Walker may not be as glorious as becoming a templar, but at least it paid well . . .

Dom was debating whether he'd spend his overtime credits on a new book or send them back home to his family when he heard some bubbles rising to the surface just off his starboard side. One of the gentle giants breaching the surface this close to the islands? It wasn't unheard of, but it was rare. But no, the bubbles were too small. Almost like someone just below the surface was gasping for . . .

As he leaned out over the side and tried to peer into the impossibly dark water, a face shot forward out of the water, gasping for air. The figure was a mess of hair, fabric, and flailing limbs.

"They're right below me! Help me. Help me for Stripe's stake, please!" Her arms grasped his as she frantically attempted to board his boat. "The judgment! They followed me up after the judgment!"

Dom barely had enough time to process what was happening, let alone take control of the situation. A woman had appeared out of the middle of the striping ocean and was ranting about demons chasing her up from the depths themselves. She was in the boat and gasping for air before he even got a look at her. Could she actually be a returned spirit? He was as religious as the next person, but he always thought the tales of rising after Depth Judgment were . . . a bit more of a metaphor. Was this woman actually in the middle of ascending to the God Stripe?

He reached out a hand to tentatively place on her shoulder. "Just breathe. You're surface-side now."

She couldn't believe he'd fallen for it. When in doubt, always just fake an act of God.

Beth tried not to think about this poor fool's feelings when she sprung up and pounced on him. She tried to avoid his eyes, but she could see them turn from sympathetic to shocked to terrified all in the split second it took her to overpower and take him down. Getting attacked by a woman who had just burst out of the striping depths was scary enough, let alone how frightening she must look with the makeshift goggles and mask she had over her face.

Portia had built the mask for Beth, and it wasn't half bad. The eye covers allowed Beth to see better underwater, though they didn't do much good in the black of night, and the mouthpiece connected to a short tube that allowed her to suck some air underwater and stay out of sight just below the surface. They always brought a pair when they were heading off island for emergencies, but this was the first time she'd actually had to wear one. As a bonus, the contraption was bulky enough to cover most of her face from the Depth Walker she was wrestling. After pinning him to the deck of the small boat, she wrapped a piece of fabric over his eyes and removed the mask.

"Don't scream. I'm not going to hurt you, and this'll be over before you know it."

Beth let out a short birdlike whistle, and Portia began rowing toward Dom's vessel.

"What are you going to do to me?" Dom whimpered. This wasn't what he'd signed up for. He was supposed to be a glorified fisherman, for stripe's sake.

"Still working that part out, pal. Let's not get ahead of ourselves. First thing's first, though, let's get out of here before your buddy circles around on the next rotation."

Beth took over the oars and began rowing the boat along their planned path. She didn't want to hurt the kid, but she couldn't exactly leave him here either. She considered a strong knock on the head, but then what? Best case scenario, the next patrol would find him and immediately know something was up. Worst case, he would drift out to sea and get killed. He may be a high islander, but that didn't mean she was comfortable having his blood on her hands.

"Don't kill me for stripe's sake. I . . . I . . . I don't wanna die. I want to go home. I want to see my family."

The poor kid sounded like he couldn't breathe.

"I'm not gonna kill you. Just shut up all right?"

"I . . . I . . . I can't breathe. I can't breathe. Something's wrong with me."

This wasn't part of the plan.

"You're just panicking. Sit up."

Beth pulled Dom off his belly and positioned him at the front of the boat, seated on the floor, facing away from her. She continued rowing as he clutched the frame on either side. Beth wasn't a stranger to panic attacks. She'd had them since the day she lost her sister and mother. She knew that breathing was the key. If she didn't want their cover to be blown, she'd have to help talk him down the way Portia had done for her so many times over the years.

"I'm not going to throw you overboard. Seriously, relax. Take some deep breaths. What's your name?"

His grip tightened.

"I don't want to die out here. I won't say anything, I swear. I'll just keep circling and never say a thing."

Beth actually considered the offer. She believed he meant it right now . . . but that might not be the case once he was free. It was too dangerous. They had to keep him around until they were clear of the water for sure. Even once his shift ended, a Depth Walker not making it back wouldn't immediately mean their cover was blown. Bad things happened to these sailors all the time out here, right? He could've gotten off course, been swallowed by a depth monster, or who knows what else. But if he was there to tell his story, they'd never make it back onto the island. Security would be tighter than ever. No, they needed to stay under the radar.

"I believe you." She tried to sound calm. She wasn't.

There was silence for a few moments, as the prisoner's breathing slowed for the first time.

"Dom. I'm Dom, from Charlie."

"All right. Just keep your cool, Dom. You'll be back on Charlie with the other highborns before you know it."

Portia managed to catch up, and the pair of vessels rowed away from the islands together in near silence. Portia nodded to the sobbing blindfolded guard on the ground with a *What the stripe do we do with him?* look.

Beth just shook her head and kept rowing. One problem at a time. First get away from those other patrols . . . then figure out what to do with Dom.

Interlude 1
Moira Vex's Lament

Moira crawled into her daughter's bed while the moon was still high and held her little girl close through the sleepless night. She looked up to the stars and searched for a constellation that might signal a good omen but found no comfort or strength shining down that night.

It seemed like only yesterday their roles were reversed and Sylva had been slipping into her blankets each night. She was an independent girl, but when the sun had set and the world quieted down, she always wanted to be close to her mother. Moira held onto those nights as long as she could, but time passed and eventually Sylva slept through more nights in her own bunk than not.

As she listened to her daughter's calm breathing, Moira thought through it all again. Desperately seeking a loophole or exit strategy. It wasn't too late to run. To pack their bags and head out into the wild. But where would they go? There was strength in numbers and abandoning Sylva's duty meant leaving all of that behind. And even if they could survive out there on their own, what about the next family who lost the drawing? The next son or daughter to be pulled away from their parents' arms and sent on a doomed mission?

She ran her hands through Sylva's hair and tried not to think about the fact that this would be the last time. The last time she held her baby in her arms. The last time she could count the freckles on her cheeks. The last time she could watch her chest rise and fall and know she had done her job protecting her. After the next sunrise, Sylva would have no one to look out for her. She'd be on her own. And so would Moira. Without Sylva, she wasn't sure she could go on. Wasn't sure she even wanted to.

Sylva started in her sleep and Moira held her closer. "It's just a dream, darling. Mommy is here."

The young girl's eyes slowly opened as she stirred awake and left the nightmare behind. She pulled her mother closer and Moira tried as hard as she could to remember exactly how the hug felt. She wanted to live in that moment forever. She tried to push the passage of time away through sheer force of will and stay frozen there in those blankets. No mission, no drawing, no duty. Just her arms wrapped around her only child and the sound of bugs chirping in the distance.

Moira struggled to hold the tears in, but there was no stopping them. She had told herself she would wait. She would stay strong for Sylva and see her off without a breakdown. Sylva hugged even tighter for a moment and then pulled back and looked into her mother's eyes.

"It's ok, Mommy. I'm going to make it back." Sylva said.

Moira knew the odds. Technically there were ways to complete the mission and come back home, but those were mostly just hopes and dreams they fed to the children being sent off to get them to play along. In all her years, Moira had never seen a drawing winner reunited with their family after leaving on a mission.

"You just take care of yourself out there. Stay alive." Moira meant it. She had already given up hope of Sylva making it back home. She just wanted her to survive.

Sylva leaned her head back down on the pillow and held her mother's hand. She closed her eyes to try and fall back asleep in her own bed one last time.

"I mean it. I'll be back, Mom. I promise."

Part Two

The Swamps

It is the responsibility of each Baron to ensure the safety of every citizen of the Chain during their rule. In this task, the Baron answers only to the God Stripe itself.

—Baron Agrius

Chapter 15

Malcolm

The Baron serves the God Stripe, and the templars serve their Oaths.

—Proverbs of Templar Amaryte

The boat crashed up against a swampy shore, and the next phase of the retrieval run was underway. Aside from the brief skirmish on deck, the rest of the nautical portion of the journey had been mostly uneventful. Malcolm split up Sly and Radcliffe, as much as you could split two people up on that tiny striping death trap.

Malcolm ordered Fritz, a lanky red-headed recruit to secure the vessel to one of the massive nearby trees. The boy was no Depth Walker, but he could tie a knot better than the others. The tide would be shifting in a few hours, and Malcom reminded Fritz how important it was that the boat wasn't washed away by the time they returned.

Although there were many channels that ran through the swamps and connected to the ocean, the water was too shallow and the thicket too overgrown to travel inland with their boat. The rest of the trip would be a muddy mess until they cleared the swamps.

"Stripe! Something bit me." Radcliffe smacked his own neck as he shouted in pain like a schoolboy who fell and skinned his knee.

Malcolm turned on his heel to rip the fool's head off for drawing attention to their location, but Sly was already on him with one hand over his mouth and the other hovering over the hilt of her polearm.

When she spoke, her voice was loud enough that the surrounding recruits could hear her, but her reprimand didn't go echoing through the whole striping swamp like Radcliffe's whining.

"Mainland voices, Cliffe. The animals will hear you. And they'll rip us to striping shreds." She lowered her hand off his mouth and took his wrist in her hand. She pulled it down from his neck where it was still rubbing his bite. She was gentle with him, but he still flinched at her touch. The recent beating was fresh in his memory, and his chest still throbbed from the last time that polearm had been drawn. "It was just a blood fly. They're a lot bigger here. And there's a lot more of them. You'll be fine."

Malcolm reached the pair by the time Sly let go of Cliffe's hand and stepped back. "Raise your voice again and I'll draw a lot more blood than the striping bug, recruit. Understood?"

Cliffe managed to flush with embarrassment once again, and he shrank down a few feet at the same time. His recent status as de facto leader among the group was deteriorating with each spectacle he made of himself on their first true mission. Malcolm would be impressed if he made it back from the quest in one piece, let alone ever lived to actually earn a sword from the God Stripe for himself.

The old templar addressed the whole pack without raising his voice. "Get your striping gear together and prepare to move out. If I can hear you breathing, you're being too loud."

He turned away and stormed off toward his trunk at the rear of the boat. The auxiliary weapons and gear cache was bolted shut and locked. Nobody had a key but Malcolm—nor permission to see or handle anything inside of it. If there was one constant on Delta, it was secrets. The Depth Walkers kept secrets from the templars. The templars kept secrets from the advisers. They all kept secrets from the lower islands. And the Baron and her inner circle kept secrets from everyone. Malcolm may not have as many secrets as Tamiyo, or that snake Jonah, but as one of the oldest templars still dragging around a sword, he was closer to the truth than most.

First, he drew his steel out of the chest. The swords themselves were no secret, of course. They were so closely tied to the legend of the templars that every toddler on the Chain knew about them. The swords were rare, though. According to the myths, the weapons were delivered from the God Stripe itself so a dozen templars could protect the first Baron, Baron Prime. Those original templars had died generations ago, but their weapons still lived on and were passed down from royal guard to royal guard. The swords were reserved for the highest-ranking templars, despite what the stories said. Bards loved singing stories of hundreds of blades glimmering in the sunlight during battles from the dawn of ages, but Malcolm knew that was all fiction. There were twelve blades in existence, and he'd seen them all with his own eyes. Five were currently held by other veteran templars, six were in the weapons vault below the Baron's tower, and the twelfth was here with Malcolm. Where it belonged.

He gently pulled back the sword's sheath and took in his own reflection.

Stripe . . . when did I turn into an old man?

He quickly slid the sword back into its sheath and stood

up to loop it through his belt. The quiet scuttling of the recruits came to a stop as everyone strained to get a closer look at the blade. This reaction may have made the aging templar puff his chest with pride a decade ago. These days, his ego no longer swelled when ambition-fueled youths daydreamed about the dawn when they would take his place. As his inevitable retirement drew closer and closer, the thought of handing the sword off to someone else filled Malcolm with pure dread.

Look at these fools. None of them could handle the responsibility. None of them could protect her the way I have. They'd never be worthy of the sword.

While avoiding their reverent gazes, Malcolm noticed something that seemed out of place a bit farther into the marsh. That couldn't be . . . *a striping Depth Walker ship?* Tamiyo wouldn't have sent those netcasters inland for something this important. They were glorified sea farmers at best. There's a reason they stayed on Beta and Charlie, after all. They had been a part of her royal forces, but they could never be trusted with the kind of secrets that came along with this sort of retrieval run. No, something was *wrong*. Malcolm could feel it. Someone else was here . . . and they had a head start.

"Radcliffe, Sly. Find a dry patch of ground in this mudhole and prepare a signal fire. Purple smoke."

The pair sprang into action. At least they knew when to keep their mouths shut and take a striping order. Malcolm knelt down once more and reopened his weapons chest. He took out another case. This one was a little shorter than his sword, but wider as well. He flung its attached strap over his shoulders to secure the rectangular case to his back.

Tamiyo had asked him to bring the others back alive. When he ran into trouble this time, he was going to have more than his sword to protect them.

Chapter 16

Jonah

The Baron's duties are many. And it is your job to take as much as possible off their plate. This is what the God Stripe asks of you.

—Excerpt from the departure letter of Lord Drolt, Senior Adviser to Baron Agrius

Purple smoke. It had to be a mistake. After the lookout stormed into his chambers with the news, Jonah raced to the top of the tower to see the signal for himself. The adviser's tower within the Citadel wasn't as high as the Baron's, but it still scraped the clouds enough that he could glance to the mainland with the help of an artifact. The glass scope locked in place at the top of the tower was already fixed on the designated landing site. The purple smoke billowing up from the shore meant one thing: someone else was going for the God Rock.

Jonah descended the stairs much more slowly than he had climbed them as he decided what approach to take with

Tamiyo. He couldn't withhold this type of update, so the question was really how to direct her . . . Should she send out additional troops? Increase the lockdown restrictions and wait for another signal? There weren't many options in a situation like this. Aside from sending in backup, there wasn't much else that could be done but pray to the God Stripe that Templar Malcolm still had some fight left in him. Even if she did want to send reinforcements, who else would she trust with this sort of mission? Malcolm and Jonah had always been her closest allies in the Honor Guard, despite the fact that five other respectable and proven templars were still armed and actively serving. Some might say the Baron had trust issues, but Jonah knew precautions were a great strength. The Baron's life and secrets were too precious to be entrusted to anyone who wasn't fully incorruptible. Obviously only the best of the best should have earned the honor of becoming a templar, but the other living templars had taken their vows during Tamiyo's predecessor's reign. Malcolm and Jonah were the only two living templars she had brought into the order herself. And they were the only ones she could fully trust.

As Jonah made his way to the spiraling staircase that led to Tamiyo's tower, he passed the Heir in the gardens and lowered his head in deference to the young girl and her handmaidens. The child was wrist deep in the dirt and hardly seemed to glance up at him. He couldn't help but notice the glare from her handmaidens, though. He wasn't sure if it was because of his job history or because of the natural tension between Baron and Heir, but the nameless child's entourage never did seem to appreciate his presence. He was careful not to trample any flowers this time.

The sun was still low over the ocean as he climbed the stairs and reached Tamiyo's quarters. The guards stepped aside to make a path for him.

"She's still asleep, Templar."

"Send for some morning brew, recruit. The Baron and I have work to do."

He rapped on the door three times and braced himself for her reaction to being woken up with bad news.

Chapter 17

Beth

The Truthbringer could only lead us so far . . . Or only wanted to.

—From the journal of Aphra of Alpha, Colonel of the Truthkeepers

Beth and Portia hiked through the swamps as quickly as they could while lugging around a prisoner. So far they'd lost their life savings, Portia's store, and the right to return to their home island, and now they'd kidnapped a striping Depth Walker. This wasn't going exactly as Beth had planned.

"On your left. Watch out for those tall vines. Snakes hide in there." Beth pointed with her dagger, which she was keeping out partially to clear some of their path and partially to keep Dom from feeling comfortable enough to make a run for it. She offered Portia a handful of dried seaweed.

"I'm not talking to you," Portia reminded Beth as she sidestepped the tall vines and snatched the snack out of her outstretched hand.

To avoid having to wear the surface breathing mask to maintain anonymity throughout the whole hike, Beth and Portia fashioned face masks out of some fabric and concealed their identities with those once they had broken land. Portia pulled the lower half of it up and tossed the handful of greens into her mouth.

"What'd you want me to do? Leave him with the boat? He'd be lizard food before we made it back. I didn't have a choice!" Beth tossed her hands up in frustration.

"Hmm, I don't know. Maybe don't chase down this mission? Stop trying to get some sort of weird revenge on the Baron and her templars? Stay on our island where we have comfortable lives? Turn back when we were cut off by patrols? Don't kidnap a striping Depth Walker?"

Beth nodded as she hopped up on an enormous fallen log and reached down to pull Dom up behind her.

"Ok. So there are *some* things I could've done differently."

Dom attempted, once again, to wiggle out of the situation. "I honestly haven't seen a thing, and I don't know anything about—"

"No." Beth and Portia both cut him off.

Beth pinched her nose. She had a headache coming on, and this never-ending argument wasn't helping.

"I'll let you go once we get back, Dom. For the last time: It's too dangerous to cut you loose now. Just go along for the ride and be thankful I took the blindfold off." Beth pulled another serving of the greens out of her pouch and shoved it into Dom's mouth before helping Portia over a downed tree trunk.

"Oh, you don't want to cut him in on the score? See if he's looking for a career change? He's basically family at this point. Invite him to the crew and make sure he comes over for

Baron Prime's feast day," Portia mocked as she slapped Beth's hand away and leaped up onto the log on her own. She strode right past the two of them and took up the lead.

Beth looked to Dom. "What do you say? Wouldn't hurt to have an insider in the Depth Walkers. Portia's auntie makes an amazing steamed scalebeast for that Prime feast."

"I . . . I think she was joking. I'm pretty sure she doesn't want me to join . . . whatever it is you two are." He looked from Beth to Portia. "No offense to your auntie's cooking skills."

"Huh. We could use someone with your brains on the crew, though." Beth shoved Dom in the back, and he fell in line between the quarreling pair.

Chapter 18

Jonah

Not all heroes of the God Stripe have parades in their name.

—Excerpt from the departure letter of Lord Drolt, Senior
Adviser to Baron Agrius

"Reports from the docks came back uneventful. There are a few Depth Walker scouts still on patrol, but no indication of problems in the water there either." *Stick to the relevant facts*, Jonah told himself.

"Anything else I should know at this point?" Tamiyo was clearly displeased, but her rage wasn't boiling up to the surface just yet. Purple smoke was a bad sign, but it didn't indicate failure. Malcolm could handle this. The mean old bastard had handled everything they'd thrown at him over the years. More than anyone should have to. He would finish his mission. One way or another.

"That's all the information we have so far, my lady." No need to mention the possible . . . inaccuracy of the impact point estimate. A giant rock had fallen from the sky, and Malcolm had coordinates to put him in the general area. He'd find it. And he'd find it *first*. "The lookouts are continuing their observation, but that was just the first signal for now. I've drawn up some recommendations on how to proceed if you feel Malcolm's retrieval crew would benefit from backup. I know our reinforcements are a bit thin, but Templar Zorra has been training a very promising trio of recruits. They're—"

"No. I barely trust her to hold the bridges. You think I'd send her to a God Rock?"

"Right. Of course not, my lady. Templar Mullen has been working with—"

"Mullen? Are you striping mad, Jonah? The old religious fanatic? Do you not remember the way he wept at my ascension ceremony?"

"Tears of joy, perhaps?" Jonah suggested.

Tamiyo laughed as she leaned across the table and closed Jonah's notebook. "The answer isn't in your scribbles and sketches, *Templar* Jonah. It's sitting right across from me."

A knock at the door signaled breakfast had arrived.

"Baron Tamiyo, surely any of the active templars would be far more appropriate for this sort of mission."

Tamiyo opened the door and ushered the guard in with her platter. Warm oats, fresh fruit, and sky black morning brew. All carefully rationed luxuries that the lower islanders would never have the benefit of tasting.

"Jonah, you and Malcolm are my oldest allies. The only two people in the world I would trust with the secrets of a God Rock. And, as of late, Malcolm has been . . . less of the man he once was. Perhaps support from an old friend will remind him of the templar he was born to be. The templar *we* made him."

"I . . . don't think Templar Malcolm has any interest in receiving help from me, my lady. And besides, I'm out of practice. I haven't set sail in years, I have no battle wards." His hand went to his waist out of an old instinct he thought had faded away years earlier. "My sword is retired."

Tamiyo lifted the glass of morning brew and moved toward the rear window of her chamber. "Your sword is hanging over the mantel in my weapons cache. It's not as if it's been melted down or passed on to another. It's waiting for you."

Of course Jonah knew this already. He had placed the sword there himself and dreamed of returning to that sacred chamber many times in the years since. For his lifetime he had been trained that his weapon was an extension of not just his arm, but of his soul. The artifact was bound to him and he never felt closer to the God Stripe than on the days he had wielded it in Tamiyo's name.

"But . . . the codes. Tradition. Once a templar retires, there's no going back to the blade." Jonah reminded her.

But she'd made up her mind. He could already see there was no getting out of it.

"I rule these islands, Jonah. Not some ancient striping codes."

He would be going to the mainland again. After all those years. Back to where things fell apart the first time. Back to where he broke his vows and lost his place with the templars.

"And who will advise you in my absence? Who will have your ear while your lead counsel is off on a mission he's no longer suited for?" Jonah asked.

Tamiyo smiled across the table over her steaming drink.

"I'll be following my own advice until you return. So you better hurry up before the whole Chain crumbles into the depths below."

This was a death sentence, even if she didn't know it. If the swamp lizards and sea monsters didn't kill him, he was certain Malcolm would.

Chapter 19

Malcolm

There is no trust like that between two templars forged in the same furnace.

—Proverbs of Templar Amaryte

Tracking was *not* Malcolm's specialty. It wasn't really a skill needed very often on the islands. There were stories of the ancient templars tracking down beasts inland and bringing them back to roast over open fires, but they'd evolved beyond the need for such dangerous expeditions. There was enough fish to feed everyone on the islands when the Depth Walkers did their jobs. Coming to the mainland was a needless risk. A last resort. Malcolm had lost too many friends and recruits on the cursed land, and all he wanted to do was get the hell off it.

He may not know how to track whoever was in that Depth Walker skiff, but he knew exactly where they were going. They had a head start, but he could still fix things—

double-time it to the God Rock, clean up the mess, get back to his island. And then maybe it'd be time to hang up his sword once and for all. He always imagined he would serve Tamiyo until his final breath, but the closer he came to his judgment and ascension, the less ready he felt to face it. He just had to have one more victory. Remind her why she'd chosen him all those years ago. She would remember. She always remembered eventually.

Malcolm led the party through the knee-deep mud at the fastest pace he thought they could handle. Sly and Cliffe fell in behind him, and he had no doubt the two of them could actually outpace him at this point in his tenure. The others were barely keeping up. He held up his hand to signal a stop, and the gesture rippled back from recruit to recruit until they had each frozen in place. Good. He'd at least taught them *some* degree of discipline. Funny how all it took to knock a group of young soldiers into order was their first brush with death.

He looked ahead through the marsh, which was covered in shadows and darkness thanks to the looming trees, despite the high Stripe hour. He pulled the canteen off his shoulder and took a swig of water while he surveyed the party. How much could he trust them? He'd been working with most of the group for the better part of two years. He knew who was the fastest, who was the strongest, who could climb the highest, and who could blend into a crowd without being spotted. But there were some things hours in the training yards couldn't teach you about a person. He should've visited the barracks more. Taken meals with them like Templar Mullen had done with him and Jonah. Mullen's wards trusted him like a brother, feared him like a father, and loved him like a son.

Malcolm had tried that approach with earlier batches of recruits. All it brought him was heartache in the end.

So he'd done things differently with this crew. They weren't a family, they were a squad. He didn't know their parents, listen to stories about their lovers, or comfort them when they started to grow homesick. He was their commander. They feared his wrath and followed his orders. It had taught them how to stay in formation and maintain silence on this expedition, so it was working so far . . . but something still itched at the back of his mind. Could he really *trust* these children? Could they really trust *him*?

He knew a few things for sure. Sly was fast. Cliffe was eager to prove himself. And you never sent a soldier out into the wild alone.

"Sly, Cliffe," he whispered.

"Templar." The pair answered in unison with a discipline that was impressive even for them.

"Think you two can manage to stop stabbing each other in the back long enough to save this mission?"

Chapter 20

Beth

In the end I was more surprised by those who betrayed us, than those who joined our side.

—From the journal of Aphra of Alpha, Colonel of the Truthkeepers

"Did you hear that?" Dom muttered for about the fiftieth time as the trio transitioned from a fallen log onto some mostly solid ground for the first time in an hour. He was spending so much time staring at the mess of branches and vegetation over their heads that he had tripped a half dozen times and nearly fell face first into the swamp at least once.

"You know, I would've thought a Depth Walker would be a lot braver. Standing on top of damnation all day, wrestling Depth beasts? That stuff sounds a lot scarier than a stroll through the swamp to me," Beth said.

"You've already kidnapped the poor guy, can you not tear his identity apart too?" Portia still wasn't happy with Beth, but she was at least acknowledging her presence. It was a step in the right direction.

"I'm just saying, it's not as bad as people think it is. Stay out of the swamp water, don't walk through the tall grass, and don't let any flying monsters carry you away," Beth said as Dom looked up to the branches again. "It's a lot easier than Depth Walking if you ask me."

"You're hilarious for a kidnapper."

"Aw, I think he likes me," Beth teased in a vain attempt to get Portia to laugh.

"But people really do get carried away by monsters here. Last winter a whole crew came in for a hunting exercise, and only one templar made it back to the Chain alive. And those were trained recruits with real weapons. Your cute little coral spear isn't going to do us much good when the monsters find us. Especially when I can't even defend myself." Dom held up his bound hands in frustration.

Beth moved up beside him and flung an arm over his shoulder.

"Don't worry, Dom. I'll protect you if the big bad monsters find us." She flexed her bicep with her free arm.

"Always so chivalrous. Don't trust her, Dom. She'll betray you the second some shiny treasure catches her eye." Portia came to a stop as they reached another extra muddy portion of swampland.

Beth looped an arm through Dom's and rested her head on his shoulder as they stopped beside Portia.

"She's lying. You're the only shiny treasure for me." She gently booped him on the nose.

"I've changed my mind. Can I go back and wait for the lizards to eat me in the boat?" he asked.

Beth looked around and tried to orient herself. They'd covered a lot of distance already and should've been able to make it to the crash site before sundown. Assuming they could find a way around the death pit.

"Go around?" Portia suggested as she looked down the side of the swamp channel trying to spot a break or a turn.

"I'm not seeing any end in sight. If we wind up walking chains out of the way to get around this, then the official retrieval crew could beat us to it."

"The gap has to be . . . thirty lengths? Even if we drag over a downed log, it's too long to make a bridge. Go through?" Portia suggested.

Beth walked up to the water and plunged her spear into the dark, thick surface. "It's pretty deep."

"Listen, you don't want to swim in that muck. Seriously. Look!" Dom gestured halfway across the water where something rippled just below the surface. "You know what that is, yeah?"

"Stripe that. We go around." Portia agreed as she backed away from the water. "Let's head this way. There's got to be a break down there before long. We'll just double-time it."

Dom didn't need to be told twice. As he and Portia started walking along the side of the channel, Beth worked through an idea and looked up at the trees blocking out most of the sunlight overhead.

"Hang on . . . there might be a faster way."

Dom and Portia exchanged a worried glance and followed her gaze to the skies.

Chapter 21

Jonah

Your career path has been . . . less than traditional.

—Excerpt from the departure letter of Lord Drolt, Senior Adviser to Baron Agrius

For the first time since his retirement, Jonah took the winding stairs down to the Baron's weapon cache. During his days as a templar, protecting these treasures and weapons was one of his primary responsibilities. At that time, he and Malcolm made a name for themselves as the Baron's most trusted servants. That didn't sit well with some of the older templars who'd spent decades serving Tamiyo's predecessor, but they would never dare to question a Baron's judgment. That's why those who were still alive were off guarding bridges and walls and he was here living comfortably in a castle. Tamiyo assured him that he'd earned his place as adviser, and he'd earned his retirement, despite what

Malcolm and the rest of them thought. So what the depths was he doing opening this door again?

It was hard for Jonah not to think of this as some kind of revenge from the God Stripe. He'd made mistakes; he'd hidden things from the Baron. And the Baron was the voice of God on the islands. So now he was being punished. Forced to wield a sword again and head off to his death on the mainland. A place he swore he'd never return to after his last visit earned him nothing but shame.

The guard outside the weapons cache looked as surprised to see Jonah as he was to find himself there.

"Open her up, recruit. Baron's orders."

Although opening the cache was something only the Baron herself or the Templar of Lore and Artifacts were allowed to order, the young soldier didn't hesitate in drawing a key off his belt and heaving the massive door open. It might have been because of Jonah's place as Tamiyo's right hand, or it might have been because there hadn't been a Templar of Lore and Artifacts on the islands since Jonah retired from the position. Although each sacred templar duty should always be filled, Tamiyo simply didn't trust anyone but Jonah to handle these sorts of secrets. Well, aside from Malcolm, but he wasn't interested in this particular duty. "Babysitting a room of artifacts," as he liked to call it, wasn't exactly how Malcolm preferred to serve the Stripe. But that didn't mean he wouldn't visit the cache before a particularly challenging mission to find a bit of additional God Stripe gifted weaponry.

Jonah entered the room and rushed beyond the crates of weapons and armor all around him. He went straight for the corner of the room, where his sword was hanging. With so few true swords available, it was a wonder his was still in storage. Tamiyo had multiple opportunities to pass it on to a younger templar, but she had yet to find anyone worthy of wielding the steel and carrying on Jonah's legacy. She was going to have to learn to trust someone else sooner than later. Jonah and Malcolm were both aging quickly, and swinging swords was a young servant's calling.

The sheath for the sword lay on a nearby mantel, and Jonah could've sworn he remembered setting it in that exact spot the day he came down here to make his retirement official. Tamiyo may have occasionally escorted Malcolm into the chamber to resupply for a birding hunt or for more weapons for his quickly dwindling pool of recruits, but the regular maintenance of the room had long since been abandoned. Piles of dust collected on priceless artifacts as one last layer of cover over the ancient secrets.

Jonah reached above the mantel and pulled his steel down from its place on the wall. It was heavier than he remembered it being. The blade hadn't taken as many lives as Malcolm's or even Zorra's, but it had done enough damage in its own way. He reminded himself that carrying this weapon didn't make him a templar again. That life was still behind him. It was just a tool. A tool he'd hopefully not even have to use.

He rammed the blade into its sheath and spun around to leave the room. He stopped a few strides before the door as he noticed one crate where the dust didn't lie quite as thick as on the others. He threw the lid open on the long, heavy storage device and cracked a smile as he saw the empty recess where one of the weapons should be.

So, Malcolm has started to see the value in artifacts, after all . . .

Chapter 22

Sly

She was barely a child, and already they began her training.

—The case of *Moira Vex v. The Council of War*, opening statements

You didn't need to be any kind of trained tracker to follow this band of idiots. That was only partly the fault of the careless criminals and mostly due to the terrain. Covering up tracks in knee-deep mud wasn't exactly an easy task. It worked out well for Sly and Radcliffe, who were able to follow the muddy imprints without any concern about losing their backup. They would follow the criminals' bootprints, and Malcolm would follow theirs.

She needed this to go well. There was no margin for error out in the swamps. And she needed Malcolm's trust. His full trust right up until the end of this mission. If that meant swallowing her disgust for Radcliffe's particular brand of bravado and stupidity, she could handle it for a few hours. She'd even try her best to keep him alive.

Unfortunately, the good behavior that Radcliffe had been

frightened into through Malcolm's rage and the unfamiliar setting were starting to fade as the pair ventured farther from the templar. Radcliffe clearly no longer felt like his life was in immediate danger. He was slipping back into his usual habits.

Now would be a great time for a swamp lizard to charge out from the brush and remind him where the stripe we are.

"This way. Stay quiet, I think we're gaining on them." She whispered.

"He didn't put you in charge, you know," Radcliffe snapped back as he stopped to pull his flask off his hip and have a drink.

This boy . . .

Sly stopped and took a deep breath. She thought back to her training and couldn't recall any lessons on how to handle privileged, overconfident men who thought the world should be handed to them simply because they showed up. "I'm not trying to boss you around, but I'm also not going to let you stripe this up. He asked us to scout ahead because he knew we wouldn't need breaks like the others. So, either drink while you jog or don't drink. But we're not stopping until we're on them."

"Well, we might be stopping anyway, unless you brought a striping boat in that backpack." Radcliffe pointed over Sly's shoulder to the clearing ahead of them. They stepped forward through the brush and found a mess of tracks near the edge of a channel of water. The path stopped here.

Chapter 23

Beth

Not every soul on Delta knew the lies, but some of the rebellion believed they should all pay. Even me.

—From the journal of Aphra of Alpha, Colonel of the Truthkeepers

"Try not to look down" is always what people say when someone is nervous about heights. But not looking down wasn't exactly an option when you were on your hands and knees climbing from branch to branch across a forest. Beth wasn't exactly scared of heights; she'd been jumping around rooftops on her island and scaling the side of the stacks for as long as she could remember. No, it wasn't the height that bothered her so much as what was below. Falling into a disgusting pool of mud full of hungry swamp lizards, snakes, and stripe knows what else sounded a lot worse than smacking into the roof of a lower stack. She'd take a sprained wrist or ankle over becoming swamp food any day.

The good news was there were no birds in sight. Portia just wanted to get this mess of an expedition over with, so talking her into climbing up the tree wasn't as hard as Beth expected. Dom, on the other hand, was a bit more of a disaster. She agreed to unbind his hands for the climb, though, so wasn't this a good thing for him? Somehow he still didn't see it that way.

The initial ascent wasn't bad, really. Beth and Portia had been scaling the stacks back on the Chain since they could walk. Trees in the swamps were enormous, and every dry patch of land was overcrowded with them. Getting up to the first branch was a bit of a challenge, but Beth was able to stand on Portia's shoulders and reach the initial landing. From there, Portia sent Dom up despite his pleas, and Beth helped pull Portia up last. The massive trees were cluttered with thick, sprawling branches, and after climbing just ten or so lengths upward it was hard to tell which trees the branches even belonged to. Heading away from the trunks and out over the channel . . . that's where things got a little tougher.

The branches were thick enough to hold their weight, as long as they stayed spread out a bit, but they were a little less abundant closer to the middle of the channel. The branches from either side of the body of water did meet in the middle, but it didn't quite form the solid ground for walking across that Beth had sold Portia and Dom on. Still, it was going to be way faster than finding a way around the channel and much safer than swimming through it.

Beth had stopped and was assessing the best path forward to the next branch when she heard Portia softly let out a bird-like whistle. For the first time since they'd come up with their code, Beth hoped the sound didn't too closely resemble something that might attract any actual birds to their location.

She hesitantly craned her neck to see what Portia was trying to tell her and found her partner pointing down below, near the bank of the channel. Beth froze in place. Two striping templar recruits had caught up to them.

Chapter 24

Sly

I sang her to sleep the night before they came for her. She was young and hopeful enough to believe it might not be the last time.

—The case of *Moira Vex v. The Council of War*, opening statements

"I don't get it. The path just . . . stops." It didn't make any sense. Sly could see the tracks they were following continued a few paces down the channel, but didn't keep going that way. It almost looked like they turned around and headed back into the thicket. But if that was the case, they would've run right into them, right?

"They went in the drink. It's obvious." Cliffe took a knee as he looked out across the water.

"If they did, then they're dead," Sly declared. "You think the Depth monster stories are scary? I'd go deep sea swimming in the ocean any day over a dip in these dark waters. They're full of lizards. It's a death sentence."

"How would you know? You've been here as long as I have. Those could just be scary stories from whatever lowborn stack you grew up in."

"I just . . . it's just a feeling. These waters are bad. Besides, doesn't it look like they turned around?" Sly tried to redirect Cliffe's attention away from the channel and back to the clearing where the tracks got messy. "Something's not adding—"

"UP HERE! HELP!"

The shouts came from above and were silenced and replaced with a flurry of twigs and branches falling to the surface of the water as quickly as they started. Cliffe looked up at the mess of branches sprawling over the channel and laughed. He clearly didn't notice the ripples near the surface of the water where the twigs and branches had landed.

"I think they need our help, Sly. The heretics got themselves stuck."

Chapter 25

Beth

The Stripe was more than just our God. It was our history.

—From the journal of Aphra of Alpha, Colonel of the Truthkeepers

Dom . . . *after all we've been through together.*

Beth pounced at the Depth Walker and threw a hand over his mouth the second he started shouting, but it was already too late. Their cover was blown. She should've kept him gagged out here. Or left him tied up in his boat to gamble with the creatures. This whole job had been a mess from the start, and now there was no turning back. The team below may not have any swords she could see, but they were still a striping Citadel Retrieval Crew. She and Portia would never make it out of this alive if they got caught. Best case scenario would be a dungeon cell in the bowels of Charlie, but this was heresy. They'd be sacrificed to the depths for judgment if she didn't find a way out of this. No trial, no jury. Just a dark, watery, and early grave.

"I really wish you hadn't done that, Dom. We had a good thing going up here. I shared my seaweed with you, man!"

Portia crawled up beside Beth, who was still holding Dom down with a hand over his mouth as twigs and branches fell to the surface below them.

"We leave him and make a run for it."

"But they know where we're going."

Portia shook her head. "Not if we don't go for it."

"But—" The possibility of giving up hadn't even crossed Beth's mind.

"They have to go for the rock. We don't. Dom hasn't seen our faces, and the Retrieval Team won't catch us if we make a break for the islands now. We can still get away. We don't have to die for this."

She was right. She'd been right since the beginning. The God Rock was an impossible dream. The Citadel didn't want anyone else near the crash sites, and there was no way they could've outrun a team of templars. Even if they did manage to make it there first, Beth had no idea what they were looking for. She just knew the Baron wanted it, so it must be important. And she loved the idea of taking it from her. She shouldn't have it all. She should know what it's like to lose. To have something she loves taken away.

Beth could let this go. Portia was more important than the score or the chance to burn the Baron and the templars. This wasn't going to bring her mom back. Wasn't going to bring her sister back. Wasn't going to make her dad the man she wished he would be. Portia was still here though. Her life was more important. She could swallow her pride and fix things with Mitch. She could get them back on the island before anyone even noticed they were gone.

Beth opened her mouth to agree with Portia, but all that came out was a gasp as she heard the crack of a thick branch snapping and saw Portia drop out of sight.

Chapter 26

Sly

A life of lies is no life at all.

—The case of *Moira Vex v. The Council of War*, opening statements

Sly was sizing up the tree trunk and deciding how she would explain her climbing skills to Radcliffe when she heard the snap. The mess of branches overshadowing the channel was only about fifteen lengths up by her estimate, so the impact certainly wouldn't kill whoever came crashing into the water, but it wouldn't need to. The monsters lurking below the surface would take care of that.

Sly and Radcliffe spun around to find some twigs and branches crashing to the surface and a woman hanging above the water, barely gripping onto a second person's hand. The woman's face seemed to be covered by some kind of fabric mask, and her clothes were blanketed in mud. Sly couldn't get a great look at her, but at first glance she didn't seem like much of a Depth Walker. Even if they were mostly disguised by swamp muck, Sly could see that outfit for what it was: low-island rags.

Cliffe stood at the bank of the channel at a loss. "What . . . what do we do?"

Oh, now he's ready to take orders.

"Wait here until she drops. I'm going up."

"What?! Why?"

Sly was already halfway up the trunk and to the sprawling branches by the time the question was out of his mouth. She shouted back down to him before disappearing into the overgrowth.

"Stand guard and watch what happens if she falls. I've got to go track whoever else is hiding in case they make a run for it."

Chapter 27

Beth

We couldn't reach high enough to pull the God Stripe crashing to the ground, so the Baron's tower would have to suffice.

—From the journal of Aphra of Alpha, Colonel of the Truthkeepers

It all happened faster than Beth could really process it. The branch snapped, Portia disappeared, and she felt Dom become a lot heavier as his arm reached down to take hold of Portia. Now here they were. Portia swinging over the drop. Dom straining to hold her up with just one hand. And Beth, holding on to Dom's shoulder with one hand and his mouth with the other. Oh, and the sound of something scurrying toward them.

Beth managed to gently lift her hand off Dom's mouth.

"Just hold on. I'm going to help you." She was speaking to both of them. She gently released her grip on Dom and scooted to the other side of the new opening in the branches to look down at Portia. She tried to focus on Portia's eyes and ignore the murky water waiting to swallow her below.

"Hey, gorgeous. Come on in." She reached her hand out for Portia's other arm.

"Flirt later. I'm losing my grip here." Dom held on to Portia's wrist as well as he could, but she was slipping.

Portia swayed a bit for momentum, which caused another terrifying creak from the branches holding Dom in place as she reached her free hand up to Beth. They connected.

"We're going to pull her up, Dom. Get ready."

"Stop." A dark-haired woman in a templar recruit uniform stood on the branches a few feet away from Beth. "Make a move and I stomp." She stood with one foot raised over a cluster of branches.

"What the stripe is going on up there?!" a man's voice bellowed up from below. Portia was starting to lose her cool.

"All right, your highness. You got us. Just let us pull her up." Beth said. All that mattered was saving Portia now. They could come up with a way out of this later.

"You'll pull her up when I say and how I say. Otherwise all three of you are going to be lizard food."

The branches below Dom let out another creak.

"For stripe's sake, screw this!"

The look of panic in Dom's eyes was the last thing Beth remembered before everything went wrong. He tried to yank Portia back up through the hole, but his movement and tension were too much for the branches. Before any of them had a chance to act, a chain reaction of cracks and snaps rippled through the trees, and the one-person-sized hole Portia had fallen through grew four times bigger. Portia, Dom, Beth, and their new friend all tumbled through the hole and plunged into the murky swamp.

Before she smacked into the surface, Beth could've sworn she spotted someone on the shore jumping into the water to join them.

Chapter 28

Jonah

Forget everything you know about problem-solving in the heat of battle. The steel will do you no good in this tower.

—Excerpt from the departure letter of Lord Drolt, Senior Adviser to Baron Agrius

He had his weapon, now Jonah just needed allies. He debated which of the old guard to go to for help, but at the end of the day there were simply no good options. A third of the templars were jealous of his proximity to Tamiyo, a third didn't trust him after his falling out with Malcom, and the rest would surely send spies or backstabbers onto his boat.

The Order of Templars had never exactly been a true brotherhood without secrets or scandals, but from what he was told, things were a lot quieter before Tamiyo's reign. Many of the older templars didn't appreciate Malcolm and Jonah's accelerated rise through the ranks, but they could've lived with them becoming templars. It was Tamiyo's refusal to trust any of the veteran templars that rubbed them the wrong way. Many of the people serving during Tamiyo's predecessor's reign had been reduced to glorified bridge guards after the transition, while Jonah and Malcolm were handed sacred duties they hadn't earned the right to protect. That didn't leave Jonah with many friends in the years that followed.

There were two reasonable options to fill out the rest of his makeshift crew.

He knew Mullen wouldn't say no. In truth, none of the templars could really say no to a direct order from the Baron, but he needed to go to someone who would actually provide him with some recruits who could handle a difficult situation. Mullen was the best of the old guard. He'd treated Jonah like a son in those early days and never questioned his worthiness. Instead, he'd just tried to help Jonah become the kind of man he needed to be in order to handle the weight that had been placed upon his shoulders. Mullen's recruits would be trustworthy and well trained. But Jonah hadn't spoken to Mullen since his falling out with Malcom. When he had orders to send to Mullen's squad, he always used a messenger. He wasn't ready to face his old leader. Not yet. And especially not while carrying a sword that he had retired.

So, no, he wouldn't be going to Templar Mullen.

That left Templar Zorra.

Zorra was one of the few templars Jonah considered as honorable as Mullen. She had a reputation for bloodlust, but Jonah knew those were just stories bards sang to earn coin. She had spilled more blood than any of the other templars, that was true. But that was simply the result of her skill. She had always wielded her weapons with honor.

Jonah knew her recruits would be ready for a fight. And something told him that's what he was going to find when he reached the mainland. Ultimately, Zorra fell into the category of old squadmates who didn't trust Jonah after his falling out with Malcolm. He could handle that, though. He'd rather face her scorn than Mullen's disappointment.

As expected, he found Zorra at the training grounds. Her recruits were running sparring drills while she paced around their formations and watched with a critical eye. Her long, braided hair fell down nearly to her waistline. The style hadn't changed since they had trained on that same field together, but it had grown more than a few inches.

Jonah stood up tall and tried to remember how to carry himself across the yard like a templar. The look of shock on Zorra's face had turned to worry by the time he reached her.

"Is it still heresy to break the Templar Oaths if the Baron asks you to do it?" She asked.

"The Baron's voice is the voice of the God Stripe," he answered almost too quickly. He'd asked himself that same question too many times. "Besides, Baron Prime wrote the Templar Oaths. What's to make the Baron of our age any less qualified to . . . adjust the rules?"

Zorra kicked at a recruit's foot to widen their stance. "Wider. Lower. That's where your power comes from."

They continued walking while she offered notes and critiques to other recruits. Wider stance. Eyes ahead. Follow through your swing. He'd heard her give the same advice for a lifetime. It never stopped being relevant.

"So, I assume your return from retirement has something to do with the latest God Rock?"

"It does, unfortunately. And I'm going to need your help."

Zorra leaned her head back and let out a laugh.

"Well, that's rich. Senior Adviser to the Baron and legendary Templar of Lore and Artifacts Templar Jonah needing help from a lowly old bridge guard like myself. I think you'll find I'm quite busy at the moment."

"Zorra, it's Malcolm. He needs us."

She hesitated. "Nobody knows the mainland like Malcolm. He can handle a retrieval mission."

"He sent up the purple smoke upon landing. He's requested support."

Her hesitation turned to anger. "Why didn't you send us out at once, Jonah?! And this is no time to grab your old sword and try to make amends. Do you think he's going to miraculously forgive you if you show up to answer his call?" She turned to address her recruits. "Simone, Arin—prepare a travel kit. We're being deployed."

The pair rushed off. That was fine. Jonah would need them ready anyway.

"It's . . . a bit more complicated, Zorra. The Baron specifically wants *me* to go. I can take Simone and Arin. I'll protect them as if they were my own recruits, I swear. But you need to stay behind and protect the island."

Her face turned as red as her long braid, and Jonah had to remind himself not to take a step back in fear.

"Are you striping mad, Jonah? You're going to get yourself killed out there. But, more importantly, you're going to be of no use to Malcolm! You're out of practice, out of shape, and the fight isn't in you anymore." She eyed him up. "You said so yourself. Or have you forgotten?"

She wasn't wrong about any of it. His adventuring days were supposed to be behind him. He had no idea what Tamiyo thought she was protecting by sending him instead of one of the others. But there was something Zorra was forgetting.

"Templar Zorra, what is the third Oath?"

She scoffed at him. "You call on the Oaths when it suits your interests. You're no templar. No sacred sibling of mine. Once perhaps, but you spat on that tradition too."

"I assure you, these are *not* my interests. I would rather

send you. I would rather send Mullen. I would choose any of you to go in my place. In a heartbeat. But I *do* serve the Oaths. I *do* care about Malcolm's well-being. And the well-being of his sacred mission." He was letting his emotions show. The yard full of recruits had stopped, and they were watching to see how their mentor would respond. "Zorra, you know the third Oath as well as I do."

She let out a sigh of defeat.

"The Baron speaks with the voice of the God Stripe. I will act out their will until my final breath."

Jonah nodded in confirmation.

"Arin and Simone will try to protect you, but that final breath may be coming a lot sooner than you want it to, Templar Jonah." Zorra turned back to her squad. "What are you sproutlings staring at? I don't recall ordering a break! Back to it, recruits."

Chapter 29

Sly

And what do we gain for this deception? A scrap of information every decade, a relic of the old world? Is that really worth what we give up in return?

—The case of *Moira Vex v. The Council of War*, third day of arguments

When the branches crumbled and the heretics fell to the surface, Sly followed on a slight delay. Unlike the two criminals, who had been lying down and reaching through the hole, Sly had been standing up with a hand on the branches above her head. She tightened her grip as she felt the surface start to give way below her feet, but her full weight on the overhead branch brought it down just a moment later.

And so she found herself tumbling through the sky. Time seemed to slow as she watched the water draw closer. She thought about her mother. About rolling hills. About green fields stretched as far as the eye could see. And she thought about her mission. She'd come so close. But she hadn't failed. *Not yet*.

As she plunged into the water, she tried to prioritize the dangers. The other people were at the bottom of the list. They were lizard food as far as she was concerned. Getting to shore as quickly as possible was her best bet at survival. She just had to be a faster swimmer than the three heretics and she could get out. She could survive this.

The momentum from the fall plunged her down to the bottom of the swamp, and she kicked off the ground hard to resurface as quickly as possible. Despite hitting the water last, she somehow made it back to the top first. That was a good sign. A quick assessment of where she was in the water helped her determine which direction to start swimming. Away from Cliffe was the answer. She didn't see him on the shore, which seemed strange, but she didn't have any time to wonder where he'd disappeared to. She was slightly closer to the opposite side, so she took off in that direction.

Halfway back to the shore she heard the others surface behind her. Good for them.

"Where is she?! Dom—where the stripe is she?!" And then the sound of someone diving back below.

Well, apparently not all of them had made their way back to the top. Sly didn't envy anyone who was stuck below the surface, but the longer they yelled and splashed around, the better her odds were.

The sound of splashes drawing closer behind her told Sly that at least one of their party was following her out of the water. Apparently she wasn't the only one with a desire to see one more sunset. Though following her may not help on that front . . .

With just a quarter of the distance left before reaching what one could call dry land in this marsh, Sly saw the first pair of yellow eyes breach the surface. She considered changing the angle of her escape route, but another scaly head and set of eyes locked on to her from farther down the bank. And then another. There was no getting by them.

She didn't waste her time freezing in place, even though that was her instinct. Instead she began backpedaling away from the creatures. She couldn't see where she was going, but until she was sure those monsters weren't following her, she wasn't going to take her eyes off them. She passed the swimmer who had been following her—it turned out to be the male one—and watched as he processed why she had changed course. It didn't take long before he turned around and tried to follow her back across the water.

The monsters weren't moving, though. She tried not to think about what might be keeping them away and doubled her speed.

CHAPTER 30

BETH

We splintered then. Perhaps the lies were what kept us together for so long.

—From the journal of Aphra of Alpha, Colonel of the Truthkeepers

Beth batted her arms around blindly below the surface as she struggled to see anything in the dark water. It was like staring into the void of space, but Portia was down there somewhere, and she was going to find her.

She was pretty sure Portia went in feet first, and the water was at least thirteen or fourteen lengths deep, so the fall shouldn't have injured her. Even if it had, she should've floated to the top by that point.

As she resurfaced for air, Beth quickly surveyed her surroundings and sized up the situation. Dom and the dark-haired girl were swimming back in the direction they came from. Someone else seemed to be swimming toward those two. Not Portia, though. And there were no signs of a floating body anywhere.

She took in a deep breath and prepared to head back below the surface when she saw it. She'd never seen the eight-armed monsters with her own eyes before, but she'd heard the stories Depth Walkers used to scare children out of wandering toward the waters. A massive slimy arm burst out of the water, but Beth could imagine what else was below the surface and didn't suspect it was anything good.

The translucent arm, which was as thick as a small tree trunk and covered in spiky suction cups, connected with the dark-haired templar recruit girl and sent her soaring out of the water and through the air. Beth was too busy watching what the arm was holding to care about where their hunter landed. The end of the tentacle was firmly grasping Portia.

Dom managed to dodge the monster's massive arm as it slammed down onto the surface. Beth raced toward them as fast as she could swim. She wasn't going to let that thing head underwater again and disappear with Portia. She could still fix this. She *had* to fix this. She'd already lost too many people for a lifetime. She couldn't let the God Stripe's curse on her tear Portia away, as well.

She pulled a short coral dagger out of her waistband as she reached the trunk of the arm that was holding Portia and splashing around after Dom. Another tentacle had surfaced and was closing in on the Depth Walker. Someone else was swimming near where the dark-haired woman had landed. The water was a mess of motion in all directions, and things didn't get any calmer as Beth hugged one arm around the tentacle and began repeatedly stabbing it while holding on as tight as she could manage. The prickly suction cups tore into her forearm, but she bit her lip and ignored the pain as she stabbed down again. She didn't think she could do any real damage to the creature with a blade so small, but she could at least piss it off.

Beth was worried after the first stab barely elicited a response that this plan—if she could even call it a plan—wasn't going to work. It drew blood when she pulled the blade out, though. A dark substance leaked out of the wound and flowed into the swamp water. The monster could be hurt. She followed up with four more hard fought stabs. Breaking the monster's skin was like trying to cut through a solid wall of sea bones, but she somehow found the strength to pierce it. The creature loosened its grasp on Portia, and she dropped to the water. Beth plunged the dagger into the creature with all her might and pushed off its slimy spotted limb to propel herself across the murky water. She swam toward Portia as quickly as possible with her remaining strength.

The beast withdrew from the surface for a moment, but there was no way it was done with them. Beth was pretty sure all she'd done was make it more angry. Portia still wasn't moving by the time Beth reached her. She flipped Portia over so she wasn't facedown in the water and started dragging her back toward the shore.

She was right. We should've walked around. We shouldn't have kidnapped Dom. We shouldn't have left the striping islands. Don't let her be dead, don't let her be dead. This is my fault.

Beth thought about the last time she saw her mother and sister as she swam. She never saw her mother's last moments. Just saw the tears falling down her cheeks as she hugged her goodbye one last time. Beth always thought not knowing had made things worse. Never seeing her last moment. Never getting the real, final, one-sided goodbye. Looking at Portia then, lifeless and losing color, Beth realized not seeing this moment with her mother was a blessing. Her father had been right about something after all. She hated that.

During her frantic race back to the shore, Beth spotted that mystery swimmer dragging the dark-haired woman out of the swamp as well. The four bodies reached the shallows just as the beast reemerged and lashed out with its slithering arms. One tentacle grasped Beth by the foot as she was pushing Portia out of the water and onto the shore.

"No!" She spun around and began kicking at her captor as hard as she could. Her hand reached back into her belt for the coral dagger, but it was gone. She'd left it in the trunk of the beast's tentacle during her flurry of stabs before retreating.

"Let her go! LET HER GO!" Beth thought help had arrived when she heard the voice shouting wildly, but it turned out she wasn't the only one about to be dragged below the surface. To her left, a young templar recruit with a shaved head and an athletic build was hacking away at another one of the beast's slimy limbs as it tried to drag the dark-haired girl back into the water. His weapon was doing slightly more damage than Beth's little dagger had done, but it didn't look quite as powerful as the swords she'd heard about in tales of the old templars.

Beth turned her attention back to her own problems and attempted to find something to hold on to, since clearly she couldn't kick her way out of the beast's grip. Instead, she'd anchor herself to some roots or whatever else she could grab and then try to squeeze her leg free. She hadn't seen the creature's maw yet, and she'd prefer to keep it that way. The problem was she was still just a bit too far into the shallows to connect with the roots and large rocks at the shore. She stretched her arm out as far as she could, but it still wouldn't reach. The monster gave a quick tug, and she found her head below the water once more.

Everything went black. For a moment, Beth thought she was going to break free. The grip on her leg loosened once she was underwater, and she immediately tried to race up toward the blurry light of the surface above her head. The relief was short-lived, though. The arm quickly took grasp of her again, this time by the torso. The beast began twisting its grip tighter, and Beth thought she might actually pop. She tried to scream, and filthy water raced into her mouth and down her lungs. She didn't care. She silently screamed as hard as she could while kicking and punching the tentacle. And then . . . release. She felt the pressure on her stomach and chest disappear, and she was left floating just below the surface. She knew she should swim up, but her instincts were failing her. She was frozen.

The next thing she knew, something else grabbed her. This time the grasp came from above, not below, and it felt a lot more human. She was pulled out of the water and tossed onto the shore by Dom. He may have seemed timid and frightened, but clearly his Depth Walker training had paid off. Beth lay there motionless for a moment trying not to think about how close she had just been to death. A few lengths away she saw the male recruit dragging a detached tentacle back to shore like a trophy. Apparently his weapon was sharp enough to not only scare the beast off, but also leave it with some scars it wouldn't soon forget. She realized that he might be tossing her in a cell before long, but at this moment she owed the young man her life.

Beth snapped out of her daze the moment she laid eyes on Portia. She raced away from Dom, who was still kneeling next to her catching his breath. Beth dropped to the ground next to Portia and began crying and pounding on her chest with her fists.

"Wake up! Wake up, breathe!"

Portia's lips were turning blue. She'd been under too long.

Beth was thrown aside once more by Dom, who had only taken a moment to catch up with her.

"You're not helping." He was still catching his breath, but

his voice was calmer than it should've been after what they'd all just been through.

He tilted Portia's head back and listened for a sign of life. Beth could hear him muttering a count as he went to work breathing for her and pumping her chest. After a few rotations of breathing into her mouth and the chest pumping, he leaned down to listen for breath once again.

Breathe. Just breathe, Portia.

"She's blue. You're not bringing her back." The young male templar in training was checking on the other, his friend. She hadn't fully recovered, but she was definitely in better shape than Portia.

Dom went back to pushing on Portia's chest, and on his fourth compression she choked up a mouthful of muddy water and began gasping for breath. Beth rushed to her and knocked Dom into the muddy shore as she threw her arms around Portia.

"I hate to say I told you so . . ." Portia managed to cough the words out between gasps of breath.

Beth couldn't help but smile. "You're always right. I should probably listen to you more often."

Beth turned her gaze to Dom, who was kneeling on the ground next to them, somehow looking relieved his kidnappers were safe and sound. "That was impressive."

"Depth Walker basic training. We have a lot of near drownings. She's gonna be okay." Dom looked to the pair of armed templar recruits who were now standing over the trio. "For now, at least . . ."

Chapter 31

Malcolm

What is a templar without an Oath?

—Proverbs of Templar Amaryte

The bugs were worse this time of year. Malcolm had made his fair share of trips to the mainland, and he was known for being able to navigate the marshes better than anyone else, but he'd never get used to the striping blood flies. Or the incessant buzzing that signaled their presence before each bite.

Malcolm and his remaining recruits weaved through a patch of unavoidable tall grass while following Sly and Radcliffe's tracks. They were messy and heavy-footed, just like he had asked them to be. Staying on their path wouldn't be a problem.

As the squad began approaching a clearing, Malcolm heard the distinct sound of Radcliffe's noisy voice. The whole damn swamp probably heard it.

"Stay the stripe where you are. Don't even think about standing up, or I'll finish what the swamp beast started." Malcolm signaled a hold to the rest of the recruits as he edged closer to see who Recruit Radcliffe was screaming at.

Bless the God Stripe. They actually pulled it off.

The old templar silently glided into the clearing and found Radcliffe and Sly with weapons drawn, standing over three prisoners. He breathed a sigh of relief and signaled to the rest of the squad that it was safe to follow him forward.

"You're still too loud, Radcliffe, but well done, you two." He drew his sword as he stepped up between his recruits to get a closer look at the culprits. "What have we here?"

"Templar, if you could just—" The only prisoner in a Depth Walker uniform started, but Cliffe silenced him with a jab from his weapon.

"These three heretics almost got us killed." Radcliffe was drenched, covered in mud, and clearly at the end of his patience with the mission.

"Sly?" Malcolm looked to the more level-headed recruit for her side of the story. He adjusted his stance and held his sword at the ready. Partially to see how the heretics would react and partially because he'd taken note that none of them were bound. He wasn't about to take a surprise dagger to the eye by some Depth Walker traitor.

"I fell into the channel because of them. Nearly got torn apart by a *striping* tentacler." She paused to look at Cliffe. "I'd be dead if Cliffe hadn't hacked away at it and sent it back below."

Cliffe nodded to Sly. "Tentacler? Didn't realize they had a name."

Sly shrugged. "Just . . . seems appropriate, no?"

Malcolm may have been on to something sending them ahead together. Clearly this hunt had helped them overcome their tension. He may not be Templar Mullen, but there was still some hint of the leader he used to be left.

"So, how do you think our Baron will feel about a Depth Walker going rogue and leaving the restricted zone without permits? Especially the night of a God Rock sighting . . ." Malcolm pointed his sword toward the boy in uniform. "You. Speak."

"Dom Wallace. Charlie-born. I was sent out on a patrol, and these two ambushed my vessel and forced me to guide them to the mainland. I'm not a heretic, I'm a striping prisoner . . . Templar."

"He's a liar, Templar Malcolm." Cliffe spoke with certainty. "He was running through the swamp with them." Cliffe pointed down to the heretic who apparently had drowned. She looked like depths, but had regained her color. "And he saved that one from drowning. Used his God Stripe-given gifts to resurrect her from the depths."

"I saved her 'cause she was dying!" Dom Wallace shouted back. His fear was turning to anger at Radcliffe. Malcolm watched the other heretics' eyes go to him and his sword. He could see the realization hitting them that they may have been captured by recruits, but that a true templar had them in his grasps now.

"He's telling the truth. I dragged him out here. Stole his boat, bound his hands. He was a prisoner." The young woman sounded defeated. She could be lying, but Malcolm's instincts didn't point in that direction. The way she looked at the other woman who was still recovering . . . To Malcolm it smelled like she owed the Depth Walker this truth, not like she was lying to save a member of her crew.

Radcliffe let out a chuckle and kicked a puddle of mud like a sulking child. "Absolute bird droppings." He pointed to Dom's hands. "I don't see any bindings, do you, Templar Malcolm?"

The old templar shifted his gaze from Dom to the heretic. "I do not."

"Next she'll try telling us this one is her prisoner too." He motioned toward the freshly resurrected one, who still hadn't said a word since the full squad of recruits had arrived. "It's very brave of you. But nobody is buying your stories."

Templar Malcolm turned his gaze to the quiet criminal. She was still recovering, but should've had enough breath to speak. "You're a quiet one. Anything to say for yourself?"

"I got turned around on my way back to Charlie. Any chance you have directions to the fish market?" She coughed and spit out another chunk of mud.

Malcolm took note of the one he assumed to be the leader bracing herself to leap in front of her friend if he were to react to the joke with violence. These two were more than just a crew, they seemed like family. Malcolm allowed himself to let out a chuckle.

"Nobody wearing rags like that gets onto Charlie, young lady," he said, gesturing to her mud-logged wardrobe.

"It looked a lot better before I took a swim." The heretic was apparently well enough to jest with someone holding an ancient weapon of destruction in her face, so maybe she was going to be okay after all.

Radcliffe lost his patience once again. "There's no time for this. These heretics almost got Sly killed, Templar. They're all working together. We should get rid of them all and carry on with the mission."

"Lower your voice, sproutling." Malcolm placed a reassuring hand on Radcliffe's shoulder and looked to Sly. Whether the heretics were lying or not wasn't the primary concern. Stopping them from reaching the God Rock first was all that mattered and his top two recruits had accomplished that. He was proud of them both. Something he hadn't felt for a recruit in a long time. "Is that your report, Sly? The three were running through the swamp together?"

Sly looked to Radcliffe before responding. Malcolm could see her making some kind of decision. Perhaps considering her tenuous alliance with Radcliffe and whether she wanted to contradict him or not so soon after he apparently had saved her life from a beast. A tentacler she had called it . . . Malcolm felt like he'd heard that name before, but couldn't place when or where. It didn't matter now. He needed to get the crew moving again and reach the God Rock. This group wouldn't be the only threat to the Baron's prize that Malcolm had to race.

"What Radcliffe said. They were all working together." Sly agreed.

The old templar looked back to the trio of prisoners.

"Right, then. We know what has to be done."

Chapter 32

Jonah

There will be times the Baron asks more of you than you may think is fair. It is your duty to fulfill their wishes regardless. The Baron and the God Stripe decide what is fair, not you.

—Excerpt from the departure letter of Lord Drolt, Senior Adviser to Baron Agrius

It was nearly sundown by the time the reinforcements reached the mainland. Simone secured the skiff to a trunk near Malcolm's ship, while Arin leaped out to look for any obvious signs of distress. Jonah wasn't sure if the pair operated in such disciplined silence as an act of rebellion against his temporary leadership or simply because they understood the dangers excess sound could attract in the swamps. Either way, he appreciated their methods.

Jonah stood on the shore, looking out at the four islands towering over the ocean. If he played everything perfectly, this didn't have to be the last time he saw his homeland. He would find out what happened to Malcolm and do everything in his power to bring his old friend back to Delta in one piece. Though . . . that wasn't his primary objective. He would never admit this to Zorra, or any of the other templars, for that matter, but the Baron had been very clear. His mission here was to ensure the security of the God Rock crash site. Find out what happened to Malcolm, yes, but the God Rock came first. It was the Baron's will and therefore the will of the God Stripe.

He took note of the speck in the distance that would be the watchtower sitting atop Delta. She was there. She was watching and waiting for him to come back and confirm the mission had been accomplished. He wouldn't let her down the way others had. Jonah spun on his heel and was surprised to find Arin and Simone standing at attention just a few feet in front of him. They had their travel bags packed and weapons at their sides.

Simone spoke first. Their voice commanded the kind of respect a recruit could only master after years of training. Zorra really did prepare recruits better than the rest of them.

"No obvious sign of a struggle, but the smoke was sent up from right over here." They took a few steps to the side and bent down to poke around the smoldering remains of the fire. "Whatever trouble they ran into, they knew about it as soon as they landed. Unless they doubled back to this spot . . . doesn't look that way to me, though."

"No, I think you're right. They signaled for help right away. Lines up with how quickly we saw the smoke after Malcolm's squadron shipped out. What else?"

Arin stepped out of formation and pointed to a path leading into the marsh. "Over here."

Not 'Over here, Templar,' Jonah noticed. Perhaps a small act of rebellion amongst his otherwise textbook behavior. He didn't take offense. He didn't think of himself as much of a templar either. "Their path heading inland is pretty clear thanks to the mud. Should be easy to track them as we start. Going to get a lot harder after the sun sets."

Jonah peered into the tree line ahead of them. "I hate to say it, but it's going to be hard to track them a lot earlier than you suspect."

Arin and Simone looked at each other in confusion. They were strong recruits. Smart, too. But they'd never actually hiked through the marshes, thanks to Tamiyo's refusal to trust a squadron that wasn't led by Malcolm.

Jonah pointed up to the trees as he started to walk forward and follow the path left by Malcolm and his recruits.

"These trees get thicker and taller as we head inland. After high Stripe, the sun won't help us in there any more than it would at midnight."

Simone and Arin fell into formation behind Jonah without a complaint or question. He'd do his best to keep these two alive.

"Weapons out and eyes up. Stay close together and don't speak unless you must."

Chapter 33

Sly

*My daughter's life is worth more than your ancient espionage.
Worth more than a war that ended generations ago. Any life is
worth more than that.*

—The case of *Moira Vex v. The Council of War*, objection to plea
of tradition

"**G**o *back*? What are you talking about?"

Sly, who was usually so good at covering her emotions, couldn't believe what she was hearing. After all she'd just been through to get this far. She'd narrowly avoided being eaten by swamp lizards and a tentacler just to be sent back to the islands? This would ruin *everything*. Her one chance was slipping away.

Malcolm was taken aback by her response. He wouldn't be surprised to hear Radcliffe mouth off to an appointed templar, but Sly? The young woman was one of his most disciplined recruits. Not just of this squad, but of any squad he'd led. She realized she was slipping out of character and tightened up.

"I mean, I'm fine, Templar, honestly. I want to finish the mission. There's more to do *here*." She tried to regain her composure, but her cheeks were still red with anger, which somehow made her pale complexion stand out from the others even more. Years on the islands under the beating sun and her skin still refused to darken quite like everyone else's. She'd been teased about it as a teenager and in her earliest recruit training years. She used to allow herself to burn day after day, ignoring the pain and hoping she could force the darkened complexion on herself. No matter how many times she tried though, she couldn't change who she really was.

Templar Malcolm was already busy packing up his bag after a short break for rations. He'd decided to split the party into two groups. Sly, Fritz, and Elm would escort the three prisoners back to the shore. Night was falling in the marsh, and Malcolm insisted heading to the crash site with three extra people in tow would slow the group down too much. The leader of the retrieval team would carry on forward with Radcliffe and Metz until they reached the crash site.

"My mind is made up, recruit Sly. You have your orders."

Sly struggled to come up with an argument. A templar's word wasn't always final, but she doubted he was going to be talked out of this decision in front of his whole squad now that it had turned into a tense moment everyone was watching.

"Well, this got awkward," the apparent ringleader of the prisoners muttered. Sly shot her an unamused glance.

"Keep it shut, or you'll be gagged the whole way back." After silencing the mouthy prisoner, Sly turned her attention back to Malcolm and lowered her voice. "Templar. I want to be there with you in case there are problems along the way. I can still help."

Templar Malcolm stood up and placed a hand on Sly's shoulder this time. Much like he had done to Radcliffe earlier. She looked up at him the way she would look up at her own mother if she were standing in front of her.

"You're one of my best recruits, Sly. You'll be a templar long before the others. That's why I want *you* in charge of escorting the prisoners back. This level of heresy? The Baron will want to toss them into the depths for judgment herself. I'm trusting you to get them to her. Do you understand?"

She hated to admit it, but she did. Everything she'd done. All the hard work, the secrets, the discipline. It was all to be his right hand when the time came to chase down a God Rock. And now she was being sent back to the islands. And there was nothing she could do to stop it.

Chapter 34

Beth

No more Heirs. No more Barons. Just the Truthkeepers and those who stand against us.

—From the journal of Aphra of Alpha, Colonel of the Truthkeepers

How much good would escaping really do? That was the question Beth was kicking around as their party stomped back through the muddy marsh. A red-headed recruit with freckles and a nose that looked like it'd been broken more than once led the party. He was followed by Dom, Portia, and Beth in that order. Sly followed behind the prisoners, staying close enough that Beth could hear the sulky recruit huffing and puffing.

That girl really wanted to see a God Rock.

One more recruit followed up behind Sly. That one had shaved half of her head, and on the other side her hair grew to about shoulder length. Beth might've taken a minute to compliment her style if she had passed her between the stacks back on Beta.

Beth subtly reached her bound hands forward and scratched Portia's lower back. She didn't turn around, but Beth saw her ears scrunch up a little the way they did when she was holding back a smile.

"I'm sorry," Beth whispered. Sly was close enough to hear, but she didn't care.

"We tried." She didn't sound mad. She didn't sound sad. That made Beth feel even worse somehow.

A blunt polearm shoved Beth in the back. Not hard enough to knock her down, but enough to get the signal across. "Enough. I'm sure you'll have some time in your cells before a public judgment ceremony. You can all weep for each other then."

The motivation to avoid a harder jab in the back from Sly was enough to keep Beth's mouth shut, but Dom's temper was still boiling.

"If I spend even one minute in a cell, the High Admiral is going to have someone's head for the way you've treated me. These heretics admitted to kidnapping me, and you're still marching me around with my arms bound like I'm some kind of criminal."

Beth didn't need to turn around to sense Sly rolling her eyes. "You heard the templar, didn't you? Nobody is going to drown you until the Baron hears the full story. *If* you're telling the truth, you've got nothing to worry about."

"Then why am I wearing THESE STRIPING BRACERS?!" Dom turned around to face Sly's direction and raised his hands into the air.

Before Sly or either of the other recruits could smack Dom across the face for his outburst, the forest came to life with sound. Hundreds of birds appeared overhead out of nowhere and chirped louder than waves crashing into the islands as they soared by.

The angry red blush on Sly's face drained as her frustration seemed to be replaced with genuine fear. She raised one finger to her lips. The flock of birds carried on overhead while smaller lizards raced by underfoot. It had grown dark in the marsh, but Beth could feel the little creatures racing over her toes.

After a few brief moments the birds disappeared out of sight and the forest fell back to silence. No one in the group dared to move or be the first to speak. Beth's head was spinning as it recovered from the onslaught of noise, but she thought she heard the sound of bushes rattling a little farther up the path.

After an uncomfortable stretch of quiet, the recruit leading the party was the first to make a move. He took a step toward Dom and pointed his spear in the Depth Walker's tan face. "Not. Another. Sou—"

Before the command could be finished, a flash pounced out from behind a bush, grabbed the recruit, and seemed to storm back off into the darkness with him. Beth didn't get a great look during the quick attack, but it was some kind of lizard that stood at least three or four heads taller than the recruit. It had a tail like the little lizards that had been crawling over her feet, but this beast stood up on two legs.

The tall creature had pushed the recruit off the path and back into the darkness with a powerful kick from both legs that would've knocked the wind out of even the strongest thugs Beth had ever known. The redhead must've regained his breath quickly, though, because the screams started almost as soon as he was out of sight, and their volume made Dom's shouting seem like a whisper.

The whole group stood frozen in panic once again, until Sly sprang into action. Before Beth could even process what was happening, she felt Sly pushing her forward at a sprint.

"Run! Before the others arrive!"

Others?

Beth didn't need to be told twice. She spun around and ran side by side with Portia as they ducked under low-hanging branches and leaped over roots on the dark ground as best they could. Branches cracked, and a new voice started screaming in pain. Not Sly. Her footsteps were just behind Beth's. The recruit with the half-shaved head hadn't made it. It was just the four of them now.

Bushes rustled up ahead, and Dom took a sharp right turn into the thicket to avoid the noise. Beth considered breaking left to separate from the group and make a run for it with Portia, but before she could act, Sly had grabbed an elbow from each of them and tossed them sideways into the same mess Dom had entered.

She's a lot striping stronger than she looks, that one.

The group plowed forward, charging through the overgrown bushes and shrubs blindly. The screams in the distance faded away, and Beth was pretty sure it was only because there was no life left in the recruits, not because they had outrun their troubles.

"Here, here. Get down!" Sly yanked Beth and Portia to the ground near some large fallen trees. Dom noticed the footsteps stop from behind him and turned on his heel to see what had happened. When he met eyes with Sly, she silently motioned him to drop down. Despite his earlier frustrations with her orders, this time he complied. He took shelter behind a large tree trunk, just ten or fifteen lengths ahead of Beth, Portia, and Sly.

Beth could feel her hand shaking, but she couldn't seem to stop it. Her vision was getting blurry, and she started gasping for breath. She hadn't had a full-on panic attack in years thanks to her breathing techniques, but this disaster was starting to catch up with her. She'd led them into a death trap. It was all her fault. Just like her mom. She couldn't stop getting people hurt.

"Shut her up, will you!" Sly barked at Portia as quietly as she could while still sounding angry and terrified. Sly turned around to peek up over the side of the fallen log while Portia took Beth's hands in her own.

"Hey," Portia whispered to Beth, as calmly as someone could while they were waiting to be torn apart by the kind of monsters that should only exist in bard songs. "Just breathe. Close your eyes. And breathe."

Beth tried to slow her heart. She closed her eyes and focused on Portia's hands around her own. She thought of her sister again. Of her mother. Her heart began to race even faster as she thought about failing their memories. Letting the Baron and her templars get the best of her too. She tried to push those thoughts aside and focus on Portia. On her voice, whispering gently and fighting to hide its own tremors. Beth wondered how Portia could still be so good to her after the depths she had dragged her into. She couldn't fall apart now. They could still get out of this striping mess.

Beth's hand trembling began to slow. She wouldn't say she was breathing quite normally again yet, but she was getting closer. She opened her eyes, and her vision had returned to normal. She looked at Portia and smiled. Portia mouthed back, silently, "You're ok."

Beth's smile grew wider as a tear ran down her cheek. She opened her mouth to form a reply, but was cut off by Sly grabbing her shoulder and pulling her up to her feet. "Wrap it up, scavengers. We're moving out."

Beth and Portia were up and on their way across the clearing to Dom when they heard a sound from above that Beth had been dreading since they shipped out. The screech was loud enough to make her stop and clap her hands over her ears and cower down. When it was finished, she looked up to find an enormous wyvern craning its head and sizing up the ragged group.

Beth had gone a lifetime without running into a true monster, and somehow the last hour or two had brought encounters with three creatures she wasn't even sure existed up until today. The beast spread its massive wings and let out another roar that seemed to shake the whole marsh. Its massive beak was full of razor sharp teeth and its talons were longer than Beth's best coral spear. Its feathers were a vibrant mix of purples and gold and it might have been beautiful if it weren't so striping terrifying. Dom cowered at the tree trunk below the monster, and Portia, Beth, and Sly stood just a few feet away. The thing had seen all of them, and there seemed to be no escape. Though . . . out of the corner of her eye, Beth noticed Sly slowly backing away from the situation. Her steps were small and subtle enough to miss, but Beth felt the girl's grip on her arm loosen and then disappear.

The oversized creature leaped down another layer of branches, bringing it a few feet closer to the group.

"Run?" Portia whispered to Beth as she squeezed her hand. She was somehow still holding it despite how awkward the bindings made it.

"Not yet. But be ready." Any remaining shreds of Beth's panic were forced out by the fresh burst of adrenaline. She had a feeling whoever moved first was going to draw the wyvern's attention. She was gambling everything on that assumption.

Beth kept an eye on Sly instead of staring at the flying monstrosity. One small step after another, she was getting away. She was leaving them behind. Beth let out a tiny "psst!" to get Dom's attention. This plan relied on him staying as angry at Sly as he'd been since she'd first arrived in their lives.

Dom broke away from his staring contest with the wyvern for a moment to see what Beth was trying to tell him. She turned her eyes toward Sly and tilted her head in the same direction. Dom followed along and saw Sly inching farther and farther away. She was almost at another patch of tall grass. Beth assumed she was planning to hide out there while the rest of them became bird food. That *wasn't* going to happen, though.

He looked back at Beth in rage. Beth gestured once more toward Sly. This time a little more aggressively. She also pivoted her foot as if she was getting ready to run in that same direction. She glanced at Dom and nodded. Sly wasn't getting away alone.

Beth didn't feel good about what she was doing. Dom had saved Portia's life, and she was likely about to turn him into a snack for an ancient monster. But there weren't any other options left. Portia was family, and at the end of the day, Dom was just another servant of the Baron. She owed him nothing.

She locked eyes with Dom, who was also positioned to make a run for it. Once he looked ready, she feigned a start. Dom rocketed off toward Sly and crashed into her, taking the pair of them into the tall grass. The massive beast swooped down far more gracefully than Beth had expected and charged after Dom and Sly with talons out and ready.

After the beast passed over their heads, Beth and Portia spun around and bolted out of the clearing, vaulting over the log they had been hiding behind and racing away. Beth lost track of which direction they were heading and instead of aiming for a particular destination just tried to put as much distance between them and the screams as possible.

Chapter 35

Malcolm

Swords of Power may be retired when they can no longer be wielded effectively, but Oaths are honored until a templar's time under the God Stripe comes to an end.

—Proverbs of Templar Amaryte

Radcliffe breathed an audible sigh of relief when the remainder of the retrieval party stepped through the edge of the swamps and set foot on dry, solid soil. It was too dark to see much of the landscape in front of them, but even the first-timer recruits knew whatever was out there had to be better than what they left behind in the swamps.

"It's nice to see the God Stripe again." Metz took a knee and began digging through his travel bag for some fruit that the trio could split to refuel.

Malcolm nodded in agreement. "It's not safe out here either, but at least we can see what's coming at us."

The team wouldn't stop to camp for the night, but they did break for a quick drink and to recover from the long hike. Although Malcolm would usually break separately from his recruits, the small squad stuck close together this time. As Metz sliced the precious Delta fruit into thirds, it reminded Malcolm of his meals with Jonah, Zorra, and Templar Mullen in his own sproutling days.

Malcolm looked out into the darkness and squinted. Had he been to this spot before? He'd been through the swamps and into the rolling fields more than a handful of times in his tenure as a templar and even once or twice as a recruit under Templar Mullen, but things were so striping big out here that it was hard for him to keep track after all these years.

He preferred the islands. The tightness of them. Always knowing where the edge of the world was. Even on the days he had to patrol the teeming streets of Alpha, where people slept out in the alleys and every corner was overcrowded, he'd never felt trapped the way he did on the mainland. Since the first time he sailed to the swamps, he always remembered wondering if it's possible to feel suffocated by too much space. It wasn't something any of the other templars seemed to understand when he'd tried to bring it up around the campfire on those old expeditions. While some of his fellow recruits had laughed and teased him, Templar Mullen pulled Malcolm aside and reassured him, "Ignore them. Everyone fears something, recruit. There's no shame in that. It's a strength to know what makes your blood run cold. What matters is that you face that fear and forge ahead anyway."

Mullen helped him work through the fear, but that didn't mean he really understood it. Malcolm always suspected Mullen felt the opposite about the wide open spaces, as a matter of fact. He could see the look of wonder in his mentor's eyes every time they sailed out to the mainland. When Mullen stepped onto the swamps, anyone around could hear him take a big breath, as if he'd been underwater since his last visit.

Malcolm couldn't imagine why. The longer he was on this monster-filled and Stripe forsaken deathtrap and the farther he was from Tamiyo, the more he felt like the depths were pulling him under for judgment. He needed to get back. It was time to finish this. No more heretics. No more monsters. No more striping blood flies. He'd secure the crash site. Do what Tamiyo asked. And then he'd set his own sword on a mantle with the rest of the retired artifacts. One last success. Remind her why she believed in him.

The leader of the group stood up, and his remaining recruits followed suit. "All right. Let's finish this striping job."

Chapter 36

Beth

She's turned on us now. Some are unconvinced, but she's made her choice.

—From the journal of Aphra of Alpha, Colonel of the Truthkeepers

Beth ran side by side with Portia through the swamps long after her lungs had started burning. She had no idea where they were going. All she cared about was putting as much distance between them and the wyvern as possible.

After what felt like the length of ten chains, Beth burst through yet another tree line and gasped. Portia followed just a step behind, and her jaw dropped in disbelief. They'd been to the swamps many times on other jobs. The wood that grew on the giant trees and the mushrooms that sprouted at their trunks were useful for all sorts of things. Both were contraband, obviously, but that only meant there was an even higher demand for them. Their missions had taken them into the marshes and up a few trees, but this was the furthest either of them had ever gone inland. They'd never seen the cursed rolling fields of the Land God before.

To be fair, they could still barely see them now. The God Stripe's light, along with the clear sky of stars, did bathe the beautiful view in a pale midnight glow, but they still couldn't see everything that was out there ahead of them.

"I guess . . . we got turned around," Beth muttered as she tilted her head up to the skies.

They stood side by side and enjoyed the stripe-lit view for a few moments before Portia broke the silence. "We've got to do something about these." She held up their hands, which were still bound. "I need to go to the bathroom and it's going to get really awkward."

Beth let go of Portia's hand and reached down to her shoe. "Come on. You know I've still got one piece of coral that the wannabe templar didn't find." She slid her shoe off, pulled out the sole, and removed a small coral dagger with a wooden handle.

"They never check the shoes." Portia held her hands out, and Beth cut her free first. "What now?"

Beth looked out at the open fields for just another moment before turning back to the tree line leading into the swamps. "With our escorts to the Baron in their . . . current state . . . and that templar and the others on their way to the God Rock, I figure we can make a clean break back to the boats and be on Beta long before the retrieval team is back. Even if we wait here until daybreak to give those monsters a chance to go back into hiding, I think we'll still have plenty of time. We could even sabotage the boats we leave behind if we think we need a longer head start."

"Or . . ." Portia started.

Beth turned around to face Portia again. "Or what?"

"Well, we've never been this far from the Chain. And if the retrieval team stops to camp for the night . . . we could still get to it first."

Beth couldn't believe what she was hearing. After Mitch. After Dom. After the swamp tentacler (as Sly had called it) and overgrown lizards and striping wyvern.

"You've got to be kidding. You've been telling me this idea is insane since before we left your shop. And you were right the whole time! This isn't worth it. Screwing over the Baron isn't going to bring my family back. All that matters is that we make it back together. I can't risk anything happening to either of us. You're the only family left that really matters, Portia."

"I know. And you're right that I'm right. Like always. We've got a chance to walk away from this and disappear into the crowd. We should probably take it . . . but we've got another chance to find out what's so special about the God Rocks. I don't know . . . Now that we're on this side of the swamp, it just feels so close. We might never get a chance like this again."

She was right that they could beat the retrieval crew there if they played things just right. Beth was sure. The two of them were fast, and the templar might slow down and start taking his time now that he thought nobody else was racing to the crash site. Sure, some animals could make their way to the site and maybe disturb things a bit, but no people lived on the mainland, so with Beth and Portia out of the picture, he would suppose the God Rock was basically safe.

"We'd have to be really fast. And we're heading through uncharted territory. No idea what kind of monsters live on this side of the swamps. The rolling fields are cursed after all." Beth took a knee and looked out over the unfamiliar terrain. Trying to reorient herself after the aimless running.

"I'm ready to start running when you are." Portia pointed

into the distance. "That plateau out there on the horizon. It's faint, but I think I can see a bit of smoke. Crash site?"

Beth couldn't believe she'd missed it. She'd been so distracted by the open fields that she hadn't looked up high enough. The small line of smoke dissipating into the skyline was as clear as the God Stripe once she knew what she was looking for.

"Are we really doing this?" Beth's nerves were turning to excitement. They were so close they could see it. Nobody outside of the Barons and the royal line of templars had ever seen a crash site as far as she knew.

"Race ya there?" Portia didn't give Beth a chance to reply before she rocketed off down the hill and toward the enormous plateau.

Beth chased after her and didn't bother hiding her smile.

Chapter 37

Jonah

Even the Baron needs guidance on occasion.

—Excerpt from the departure letter of Lord Drolt, Senior Adviser to Baron Agrius

Jonah heard the first screams just as he was waiting for Simone to climb down from a tree they'd been using to scout ahead. They were making good time and hadn't run into any signs of trouble. Until then.

The retired templar signaled a staggered formation and took the point, despite the fact that Simone or Arin would have done a better job. They moved in the general direction of the cries, which only lasted for about a minute before they disappeared.

Jonah had his blade drawn, and Arin and Simone were protecting the flanks. They arrived at the first body, and Arin hunched over to vomit while Jonah leaned down to inspect the scene. The recruit was well trained but apparently had never seen what a mainland lizard could do to a person. The body had been torn to shreds, but there was enough of the uniform left to identify the victim as a templar recruit. You didn't need to be trained by the medical guild to see that this body hadn't been here for long.

Jonah spoke quietly, fearing that any sound louder than a whisper could spell their doom. "Stay. Close."

He led Zorra's recruits away from the body and back toward the main trail. He was trying to do his best to keep them alive, but even a Sword of Power was only so strong when facing down a lizard of that size. The Swords of Power were gifts from the God Stripe and had blades harder and sharper than the scrap weapons recruits were armed with. Only a true sworn templar had the honor to carry them. They were as sharp a tool as an islander could ever hope to wield, but the mainland had foes even the strongest templar armed with the best weapons couldn't stand against alone.

His plan was to get back to the trail they'd been following and start moving at double speed. Lizards were more active after nightfall, and they had to press through this area and get as far away as possible before the pack returned.

Just as they reached the clearing that had been acting as their trail, they heard the next set of screams. These were less cries of pain and more pleas for help. The sounds weren't coming from far away—just through the bushes in the opposite direction of the body they'd found. Whoever was there was already dead as far as Jonah was concerned.

Simone turned in the direction of the screams with their weapon ready. "Recruit," Jonah whispered, attempting to channel all the authority he had once wielded over his own sproutlings. "We move forward. Now."

Simone and Arin exchanged a glance. Surely they wouldn't question a direct order. "They need help. That could be Templar Malcolm and the rest of his team. Our mission

. . ." Arin stood in between the two of them, spinning on his heels every few seconds, unsure which direction they should be guarding.

"Our mission is to secure the crash site and help the original retrieval crew *if we can*. In that order." The screams continued on the other side of the bushes. "And your mission is to follow my striping orders, recruit. Would you dare disobey a sworn templar?"

Simone's face quickly turned to disgust, as if they were looking at Jonah for the first time. Maybe they'd seen him this way from the start and had just been able to hide it. Jonah wasn't sure if they wanted to know anyway.

"*You're* no templar, adviser Jonah. Not anymore."

Without another word Simone quietly skulked through the overgrowth, and Arin followed them.

They're right. I'm no templar. Not anymore.

Chapter 38

Sly

I long ago gave up hope of ever seeing my daughter's face again, but that won't stop me from fighting for the other children you use as pawns in your game.

—The case of *Moira Vex v. The Council of War*, day five of arguments

If Sly was going to die in the swamp after all the work she'd done, she was going to die fighting. She lay on her back in the high grass as Dom scurried up beside her. She'd been so close to getting away. This wyvern that could've solved all of her problems was now racing toward her with talons out and hungry for its next meal.

The winged creature descended to take hold of her and Dom, but Sly managed to ram her polearm into its underbelly and drive it back temporarily. It took to the air briefly, before landing and starting to circle its prey.

"You got another weapon?" Dom reached to Sly's belt, grasping for anything he could use to protect himself. She swatted him away.

"No." She had a smaller dagger on her side, but she wasn't going to risk handing that over. Not like it would do anything against a creature that massive anyway.

Dom fumbled around the ground and found a stick about two feet long and as thick as a child's wrist. It wouldn't have enough reach to protect him from the long beak of the wyvern, but at least he wouldn't feel totally unarmed.

The massive creature let out another shriek of anger, or maybe intimidation, as it poked its head through the grass. She could feel the hot air from its breath make its way over their hiding spot. Sly acted quickly and swung her polearm around to connect with its face. The blow landed, and the beast immediately spread its wings and hovered back a few steps. She wasn't going to deal any significant damage this way, but maybe after enough smacks to the face it would get bored and find a less resistant snack.

The next time the massive beak breached the grass, the creature was almost directly behind Sly. She had to twist around and was barely able to connect with a wild blow. The monstrosity retreated out of the grass once more, but didn't take any steps back.

Dom scrambled around Sly's side and pressed his back against hers. "Here. Back to back. Like this. So it can't surprise us."

So he wasn't totally useless after all. "You're not going to be able to do much with that stick," Sly pointed out.

"Better than nothing, right?"

The next attack came on Dom's side, and he had to lunge out with his makeshift weapon to push the monster back out of their circle. The wyvern snapped at the weapon and pulled it back. Dom tried to resist and was almost pulled out into the opening himself before he gave up and let go. The beast swung its neck around and tossed the stick off behind it. It continued circling.

"Told you," Sly said as she pulled the dagger off her belt. "Here. You're not going to have much reach. But at least you can draw some blood if she gets close." She handed him the short dagger without turning around and hoped he wouldn't immediately drive it through her back.

Dom held the blade out in front of himself and waited for the next attack. "Thanks. I'd rather not die empty-handed."

"I'd rather not die at all."

The wyvern spread its wings and hovered over the pair. It descended for an aerial attack this time and led with its talons instead of its beak. Sly thrust her polearm up as hard as possible, and the monster rolled to the side to narrowly miss the jab. Its beak reached out and took hold of the polearm before Sly had a chance to fully retreat from her attack. She held on to the hilt as hard as she could as the wyvern began thrashing its head from side to side.

Just as she was about to lose her grip, Dom spun around and grabbed onto the polearm just above her hands. He dug his heels into the ground and lowered his weight as much as possible. The beast wasn't able to swing the pair of them around like a couple of rag dolls now that they were working together, but it still wasn't letting the other side of the weapon go from its clenched jaws.

Dom shouted as his muscles strained and he felt his grip slipping. He'd dropped the dagger to the ground when he grabbed onto the polearm. Sly found herself wondering if a slash or two from that could force the creature to retreat. It had seemed to work well enough when the crazy heretic stabbed the tentacler.

Sly let go of the polearm with one hand and tried to reach down for the dagger. It was just a few inches too far away, but Dom followed her line of sight and understood what she was trying to do. He shifted his weight to one foot and used the other to kick the dagger toward Sly's hand. She was able to grasp the small blade, but Dom's shifted weight and Sly's one-handed grip had given the wyvern the opportunity it needed. It thrust its head back as hard as possible and ripped the polearm free from their grasps. The pair tumbled backward to the ground as the polearm launched out into the clearing.

Sly held up the dagger in a defensive position, and Dom shielded his face with his arms as the beast descended over them. The monster came swooping down, and the pair screamed as they kicked and slashed in a last-ditch effort to fight off their deaths. Sly didn't believe in the Depth Judgment like the other islanders, but she still wasn't ready to meet her own maker.

As she expected, the small dagger wasn't able to do much damage to the wyvern, especially with its attacks coming talon-first. A clean stab to the neck might be able to take the creature down, but she wasn't getting anywhere close to that. Her wild slices were mostly batted away or ignored by the creature as it continued an aggressive attempt to pin them both down.

Before long Sly found herself trapped on her back below an enormous talon, with Dom to her side in a similar position. They'd fought it off as long as they could, but they were simply outmatched. Sly wondered what would happen now, with her mission a failure. Would her mother ever find out how her story came to an end?

The wyvern's snout lowered down over Sly and let out another ear-piercing shriek of victory. The cry left Sly's head ringing. As she held her ears and cowered in anticipation of the killing blow, Sly spotted a pair of recruits sneaking up behind the creature. The duo wore the familiar colors of the Chain and had their weapons drawn. Sly felt a fresh burst of adrenaline as she realized the fight might not be over just yet. The beast let out another shriek, but this one was different—

this one seemed to indicate pain. The two recruits, neither of whom Sly recognized, delivered a series of attacks and caused the creature to flap its feathered wings and return to a hovering position to escape its surprise attackers.

Sly was on her feet and racing for her polearm as quickly as she could. Four on one was still terrible odds against a monster, but she'd take any help she could get. After picking up her polearm she fell into formation next to her unexpected backup and joined them in delivering overhead blows up toward the wyvern, who was hovering and plotting its next move.

"Depth Walker! Into formation!" She called out for Dom's help, but she couldn't take her eyes off the beast long enough to see what the boy was doing.

The creature may have been outnumbered, but it didn't seem to think it was at any sort of disadvantage. It charged forward with its jaws snapping. It spread its massive wings and tried to push its prey together as if to pull the whole group toward its torso for a deadly embrace. It was herding them toward the massive logs behind them. Trying to pin them down.

The newcomers were expertly trained and held their positions well. Their blows were deftly planned and landed nearly every time one of them swung towards the wyvern's torso with their weapons. They were much better fighters than her squad. Sly only had to watch them dodge, parry, and attack out of the corner of her eye to see that much. They didn't waste any energy on strikes that might miss. They only attacked when they were sure there was an opening to be exploited and blood to be spilled.

But despite the skill on display, this fight wasn't going their way. The monstrosity didn't have a lot of weak spots, and the team wasn't well positioned to get to any of them. They held their ground as much as possible but slowly found themselves inching toward the giant downed tree trunk behind them.

Sly tried to come up with a way to get out with her life and mission intact. She still had the dagger and figured one last try for the neck gave her the best odds of taking down the beast.

She called out to the other two and hoped they would listen. "Draw it your way. I'll go in for the neck."

The pair nodded and started inching away from Sly, forcing their opponent to spread its attention. Once they had a few extra feet between them, the recruit furthest away from Sly stepped forward with a particularly aggressive strike. The move left them wide open after the strike missed, and the beast turned its jaws toward the recruit to move in for the kill.

Sly could've taken the opportunity to spin on her heels and bolt out of the clearing. She didn't know these recruits, after all. They weren't a part of her mission. She should be getting back on track. That's all that really mattered to her up to that point. But still, something kept her in the fight. Maybe she just wanted to take down the creature that had brought her so close to her own demise. Maybe she would feel too guilty leaving these recruits here to get eaten alive. Either way, she dropped her polearm, charged forward, and rammed her dagger into the wyvern's neck.

CHAPTER 39

JONAH

We serve the Baron, yes, but we serve the God Stripe first. Never forget that.

—Excerpt from the departure letter of Lord Drolt, Senior Adviser to Baron Agrius

Jonah stood alone on the muddy path for a moment after Simone and Arin charged toward the screams and the shriek of another monster. He couldn't help but feel they were right. He was no templar. He didn't deserve to be carrying that blade gifted from the God Stripe. Not anymore. He may know how to twist the words of the Oaths around to always make it sound like he was the one doing the honorable thing, but deep down he knew he had betrayed his Oaths—and his friends—over and over again. There was a reason he wasn't a templar anymore. There was a reason none of the templars had trusted him in years.

He hadn't forgotten the Oaths though. One moment of

weakness and fear had haunted him for years. He thought back to his ascension ceremony. The day he became a templar. What it had meant, not just for Baron Tamiyo to put so much faith in him, but for Malcolm to be there by his side as she handed him a Sword of Power. Malcolm and Jonah had dreamed of that day for as long as he could remember. The idea of one of them truly becoming a templar would've been a wish come true. The fact that they both managed to be chosen and elevated to templar . . . it was more than either of them could have imagined.

Tamiyo had been like a daughter to him back in those early days and Malcolm like a brother. He'd lost half of that family over the years. Malcolm may never forgive him at this point, but at least he still had a chance to prove to himself what Tamiyo had seen in him all those years ago.

He looked down at his blade. He was honor bound to the Baron. He owed her everything. But he was honor bound to his Oaths as well. The God Stripe was giving him another chance. An opportunity to prove he was worthy after all. And he wouldn't make the same mistake twice.

Chapter 40

Sly

It's time for a new age to begin. Let past feuds die and forget about the sea devils.

—The case of *Moira Vex v. The Council of War*, day five of arguments

The blade sunk into the wyvern's neck, and Sly was immediately tossed through the air. The loudest shriek yet roared out of the creature's mouth as it stumbled and attempted to recover. Blood streamed down from around the dagger, which stayed in place where Sly had plunged it. When her head stopped spinning from the impact of her fall and the latest screech, Sly found the wyvern clumsily staggering towards her and trying to pin her down under its bloody talon. She had no weapons left and no time to react. The creature might be dying, but it was going to take Sly along with it.

The wyvern tightened its grip around Sly's torso, raised its torso up high, and began flapping its wings to fly away. Before it could get more than two feet off the ground, Sly saw a glimmer of light in the darkness. A figure leapt through the air towards them. The light was coming from a reflection off of a Sword of Power that was cutting through the air and Sly realized a templar was joining the fray. He rammed the whole length of his blade into the creature's torso. The templar kept hold of the blade's hilt as the wings stopped flapping and they crashed back to the ground. The sword wound was fatal and left the beast's torso gaping like a fish being gutted and prepared to spin over a cooking fire.

The beast's grip tightened for a brief moment and then loosened, and Sly dropped to the ground. It was the second time in a single day she had been saved by an unexpected hero. She found herself on her knees in a growing pool of wyvern blood while she caught her breath. She was surprised to look up and see the templar who'd swung the sword wasn't Malcolm. She assumed he'd doubled back for them when he heard their cries. This was actually no templar at all . . .

One of the recruits walked up beside the templar, who was wiping the blood off his blade with the inside of his cloak. "Glad to see there's still some honor in you after all. Templar Jonah."

"Oh, so I'm a templar again now, am I, recruit Simone?" He didn't smile, but he did seem to be jesting with them.

The recruit—the one Jonah had called Simone—helped Sly to her feet. "You going to be all right? Took quite a beating there."

"I . . . I think so." Sly honestly wasn't sure. She was bloodied, but she didn't seem to suffer any fatal blows or break any bones.

The other recruit was kneeling in the patch of tall grass

and called over to Sly. "I don't think your friend is going to make it."

Friend?

Sly found herself wondering if she had ever had a true friend. A relationship not based on deceit and half truths. Not since she'd left home on this cursed mission. She shook off the shock and stumbled over to the patch of grass where Dom was losing a lot of blood. The recruit was holding his hand over the wound, but it was too late for that. The Depth Walker's chest had been punctured straight through by one of the beast's talons. This wasn't the kind of injury someone could walk away from. Especially out here in the wild.

Sly knelt down next to him. She wasn't sure why, but she took his hand in hers.

"I . . . I wasn't lying, you know?" His voice was barely a whisper.

Sly smiled down at the boy as he drew his last breaths.

"I believe you." She wasn't sure if she really did, but that didn't matter. It was just something a dying boy needed to hear. It cost her nothing to lie. It's what she'd been raised to do.

Chapter 41

Malcolm

When the first swords were handed down from the heavens, the original Oaths were sworn.

—Proverbs of Templar Amaryte

It wasn't quite sunrise yet, but Malcolm and his squad had covered a lot of chains overnight. He knelt down and had Radcliffe spark a lantern as he took out his map for the third time. Metz stood guard and watched the horizon for any signs of danger.

"Something wrong, Templar?" Metz asked.

"Recruit, if you ask that question one more striping time . . ."

He didn't finish his thought. He'd always felt it was better to leave threats vague and to the imagination of the potential recipient.

"Right. Of course, Templar." Metz fell silent, but looked to Radcliffe in desperation.

Radcliffe held the torch steady while Malcolm studied the lines and traced their path with his fingertips. "It's just, you keep—"

Malcolm sighed in exhaustion loudly enough to cut Radcliffe off. "I keep consulting the map. I know this, Radcliffe. The estimates are . . . Something is wrong. We should be at the crash site by now. We should at least be seeing the smoke."

"Maybe we got turned around in the swamp or something?" Radcliffe wondered aloud.

The old templar shook his head. "No. Can't be. I know this exit point." Malcolm slammed a finger onto a point on the map. "I've come out of the swamp a dozen times at this point. I know it's where we broke through."

"So, maybe the map's wrong."

Malcolm actually chuckled at the suggestion. He was so sure he'd missed something. That he took them slightly off course by navigating at night rather than under the sun and Stripe. He hadn't considered this could be somebody else's mistake. Could Jonah have sent him off track intentionally? The map had the geographer's seal on it, though. Those tower-dwellers never would make a mistake like this. Could he be working with them? Trying to undermine what was left of Malcolm's relationship with Tamiyo? Draw her farther away from her most trusted templar so only the Senior Adviser truly had her ear?

"So, if the map is wrong," Malcolm pondered, "what do we do next?"

He looked out over the rolling fields. Nearly everything looked the same to him out here. Too much striping space. His head started to spin as he tried to process it all.

"We could wait until morning. See if the crash site is still sending smoke signals and go from there?" Radcliffe suggested.

The boy had surprised Malcolm twice already. Without Sly here to distract him with his own insecurities, he was proving to be a lot more useful than the old templar had ever expected.

"It won't be long before sunrise now. We'll wait and see if the sun can guide us." Malcolm approved of the plan. He hated leaving the God Rocks out there unrecovered longer than he needed to, but marching in the wrong direction would only make things worse.

Metz sat down next to Malcolm and Radcliffe and looked out into the distance. "And . . . if we don't see anything in the light?"

"I've been working with the Baron for a very long time. Longer than just about anyone, actually. If we can't complete the mission, we're better off dying out here than going back and telling her. Baron Tamiyo may be merciful enough to overlook a messy hunting party expedition from time to time, but I assure you, sproutlings, a failure to secure this God Rock is a one way trip to the depths for us all."

Chapter 42

Sly

This world is large enough for all of its living creatures. Even the islanders.

—The case of *Moira Vex v. The Council of War*, day ten of arguments

Jonah, Simone, and Arin. This was apparently the elite team Baron Tamiyo sent out when Templar Malcolm put up the purple smoke. The three of them gave Sly a moment to recover after Dom crossed over to his afterlife. She supposed taking his body to the sea would be the appropriate thing to do, but there was no time.

"So, you're saying the crash site has not been secured yet?" Jonah may have been in a rush to complete his mission, but he still made Sly run through her story a second time to make sure he understood the situation.

"Templar Malcolm was on his way to the crash site with recruit Radcliffe and recruit Metz the last time I saw him. But, like I said, two dangerous prisoners escaped during the wyvern attack. They're going to be heading for the crash site. We've got to get moving if we want to beat them there, Templar."

Jonah sheathed his sword and considered Sly's story. She was going to that crash site whether he liked it or not. Templar Malcolm could issue her an order that she had to take, but not Jonah. Not out here. Even if his authority did hold weight on the mainland, her mission was too important to be delayed again. This was her chance to get back to where she was meant to be.

"What makes you so sure the escapees won't be heading back for a boat? I'd wager you might have a better chance at catching up to the heretics if you head toward the coastline, recruit Sly. I can send Arin or Simone with you as backup and I'll carry on toward the crash site and Templar Malcolm."

Is he trying to get rid of me? Sly found herself wondering.

"Not necessary . . . Templar. I'll go along with your squad toward the crash site. You've said yourself that's the top priority now, right? Heresy is a serious crime, but completing the primary mission is what matters here. If those two really are making a run for the islands, we'll catch them when we return home. I've seen their faces. They can't hide from us forever."

If he didn't go for it, Sly planned to ditch whichever recruit she got stuck with and head to the crash site on her own. She had lost patience with the entire situation.

Jonah looked up at the trees. Sly guessed he was straining to figure out how close it might be to sunrise.

"We don't have time to debate the importance of making an example of islanders who would defy the will of the Baron, and I've learned today that recruits who are not directly under my command—" he looked to Simone and Arin, who stood at attention, "—are unlikely to take my orders in the middle of a mission like this. Because of that, you can join us as we press on. But do note that you will answer for the missing prisoners when this is all over."

Sly picked up her polearm and began leading the march out of the clearing and back toward the path. "Understood." She smiled at the thought of seeing the rolling planes again after all those years.

INTERLUDE 2
THE NAMING OF THE HEIR

Tamiyo was born to be the Baron.

The role wasn't passed down through families, but there was always a trained Heir ready for when the active Baron passed away or became too frail to continue their work. Rather than through family lines, Barons were chosen by the fates.

Part of each Baron's ascension ceremony includes the selection of an Heir. To demonstrate their trust in the people of each island, the Baron walks on foot from the gates of Delta all the way down to the slums of Alpha the morning of their ascension ceremony. While on the lowest island, the new Baron selects a child no older than six months and claims them in the name of the God Stripe.

The child is taken from their family and carried by the Baron all the way back through the gates of Delta, where they will live out their life in luxury until it is time for them to take over and continue the cycle of Barons. The tradition offers the poorest and hungriest members of the Chain hope that perhaps their child will someday rule all of the islands and speak directly to the God Stripe.

Naturally, there are many contingencies that have had to be put in place over the years to account for the potential problems caused by this tradition. The child, who is often sick and underfed from life on Alpha, can become ill and die. The Baron can fall ill and be forced to ascend to the God Stripe long before the child is old enough to take over their duties. Each of these circumstances have come to pass in previous generations, and the Baron's advisers and the Heir's handmaidens have done their best to construct appropriate safeguards to protect the future of the Chain.

The Baron doesn't act as a true parent or guardian to the Heir, so it's common for the pair to form a professional relationship. In earlier generations, the Baron would act as a direct mentor to their Heir, but this led to other unforeseen problems with certain pairings. Placing the Heir too close to the Baron resulted in more rivalry between the pair than any of the lead advisers were comfortable with. As the Heir aged and became more ambitious, some Barons felt threatened by the constant presence of the future ruler. After a handful of these pairings resulted in violence between Heirs and acting Barons, the decision was made to separate the two and only bring them together for certain ceremonies.

Baron Tamiyo obviously didn't remember being plucked out of the crowd by the former Baron, but she did remember meeting the man on many occasions throughout her youth. She recalled that he always complimented her dark hair and light skin. He said that even as an infant her hair had a beautiful shine to it. She remembered finding that strange as a young child and irritating as an adolescent. She didn't care for the way he had only seen her for the paleness of her skin or the darkness of her hair. Even as a child, she resented the way he talked about her. The way he talked to her. Always judging. Always trying to force a lesson onto her as if she wasn't also chosen by the God Stripe.

Their interactions were limited, and she knew it was best to listen to her handmaidens and stay on his good side, but she could only hear him go on about how precious a gift it was to be selected by the God Stripe for so long before she began to visibly lose interest.

When she reached her early teenage years, she used to wonder about the baby she would select. Would they dislike her as much as she disliked the man who took her from her family? She didn't remember her family or have any real idea what life on Alpha would've been like, but the life of the Heir was one of duty. It lacked nearly all manner of choice.

When the time came for Tamiyo to march through the streets and make her trek to Alpha, she tried to picture the child she would choose in her head before she got there. It was customary for a male Baron to choose a female-born child and a female Baron to choose a male-born child. This ensured a rotation between sexes and a balance in the God Stripe's plan. Despite that, Tamiyo saw the face of a baby girl when she tried to picture her Heir. She didn't picture any specific skin tone, hair, or eyes when she thought about the Heir. She just knew they'd be a girl. And she would know which one when she saw her.

Starting her rule as Baron by defying a tradition past Barons had held to for generations would certainly make a statement. Looking back, sometimes she wondered if that wasn't a part of why she felt so compelled to select a baby girl. She was going to be a *different* kind of Baron. Not like the religious zealot who had selected her. The decision caused drama from the moment she reached out for the child. To her surprise, one member of the family was willing to fight to keep the child on Alpha. An act of defiance against the Baron's will was an act of defiance against the God Stripe itself. And Baron Tamiyo wasn't going to use her first day in power to cement her legacy as Tamiyo the Forgiving.

Part Three

The Plateau

The Baron orders the sentence, the Senior Adviser sharpens the spear, but, when the sun sets behind the God Stripe, only the Honor Guard have to wash blood stains out of their robes. For that we all owe the sworn templars our gratitude.

—Baron Prime

Chapter 43

Beth

The gifts were there all along. Hoarded away. Hidden even from me.

—From the journal of Aphra of Alpha, Colonel of the Truthkeepers

The smoke had faded away to nothingness by the time Beth and Portia closed in on the plateau, but they didn't need the lines melting into the sky to find their target by that point. The plateau was massive in diameter. Much bigger than Beth thought it was when they were still chains away. Its walls were incredibly rocky and, despite their height, would be easy to scale. There were hand and foot grips everywhere. It also didn't hurt that the pair of smugglers had more than enough experience scaling island cliff faces. This would be a breeze.

"What do you think we're going to find up there?" Portia asked Beth as they started climbing side by side.

"Something *they* don't want us to have. So you know it's got to be good."

Despite her obsession with getting to the crash site, Beth had spent surprisingly little time pondering what a God Rock might actually be. The stories described them as gifts from the heavens. Direct messages sent from the God Stripe to the Baron. There were never any more details than that. Never a proclamation about what the God Rock told the Baron, never resources or food to share, and never an explanation about what any of it meant. Just a clear message that it was for the Baron's eyes alone. Nobody else on the Chain was deemed worthy enough to see the rare gifts.

Beth considered most of the myths about the God Rocks to be striping lies and propaganda. There were no messages from the God Stripe, just like there was no panel of judges waiting at the bottom of the sea. They were all stories. Tales to scare children and weak-minded adults into falling in line. But even if the stories were all lies, it was still true that the Baron cared about getting to the God Rock as soon as it fell. Whatever it was must be valuable—some kind of rare building resource was always Beth's best guess. Maybe materials from the skies that were stronger than the sea bones the bottom islanders used to make everything they needed.

When they reached the top of the plateau, it was clear they'd come to the right place. A massive trail had torn through the dirt and rock atop the surface and stretched out for what must have been at least the length of Alpha. Was the plateau really that long? Beth looked out across it and couldn't even see where the other end dropped off.

"Ready for this?" Portia smirked at Beth as they started following the trail.

"Let's go find some sky garbage."

Chapter 44

Malcolm

Don't rely on the sword so much that you forget how to use the shield.

—Proverbs of Templar Amaryte

The recruit had been right. Malcolm tried to hide his hope as they raced forward across the fields toward the small amount of smoke left streaming off the lone plateau. The geography out here was dizzying. The only thing keeping the old templar's vertigo in check was his tunnel vision on the goal. And even that couldn't protect him from what was raging across the wide open land.

"What in the depths is that, Templar?" Radcliffe pointed to the swirling mass of clouds in the distance.

Malcolm let out a grunt and began to run at a full sprint. They were fully exposed. The nearest cover was chains behind them in the swamps.

"To the plateau! We'll hide behind it until she passes!" he shouted out between breaths.

The plateau was their only chance at survival if the winds shifted and the storm decided to make its way toward them. Lightning cracked in the distance somewhere beyond the plateau, and Malcolm found himself looking up once again. The smoke was lost in the dark clouds now, but they already knew the way.

"You've got to be striping kidding me . . ." Metz pointed up as the trio approached the bottom of the plateau, but his gaze wasn't on the storm. It was on a pair of figures finishing the climb and disappearing over the edge toward what rightfully belonged to the Baron.

Malcolm looked from the top of the plateau out toward the storm. Being exposed on top of the land mass would be even more dangerous than running around down on the ground. Heading to the top now, before the storm passed, could be a death sentence. That didn't matter though. They had a mission and Templar Malcolm was not about to let any act of the Land God keep them from finishing it.

"Get ready to climb, recruits," Malcolm barked.

CHAPTER 45

THE HEIR

The world will be yours. Just not yet.

—Handmaiden's transcript of recurring conflict resolution meetings between Baron Agrius and the Heir

The Heir was digging for worms in the garden when Baron Tamiyo sent for her. Her tutors had explained that the soil was sacred and could only be found in abundance on Delta because the God Stripe favored the Baron's island. The other three islands, Alpha, Beta, and Charlie, had some dirt too. There was quite a bit of it on Charlie, or so the Heir had been told, but it wasn't as rich as the Delta dirt she was allowed to play in. She didn't know much about Beta yet, but she was pretty sure there wasn't a lot of dirt there. Alpha, where she was born, didn't really have any room for dirt at all. It made her sad to think about the children living there. They might never know the feeling of dried dirt under their fingernails or green grass between their toes.

The Heir tried to pay close attention during all of her lessons, but she often found herself daydreaming about the fields. She felt a deep connection to the dirt, the bugs, and the plants. Her tutors explained that fish and water were just as important as the soil and plants, but they certainly weren't as interesting to her. She loved watching bugs and worms crawling around in the gardens. The world must seem so massive to the tiny creatures. So much space for everything they needed.

The robed servant who came to fetch the Heir from the gardens asked her to visit a washroom on the way to the Baron's tower to make herself more presentable. As she entered the washroom, a small flock of her handmaidens sprang into action. Her trousers and shirt were pulled off, and she was submerged into a bath where the dirt was scrubbed off every inch of her. Even under her fingernails.

"Wait!" she shouted as she was being pulled out and dried off. "Get the rock out of my trousers before you take them away. Leave it by my looking glass." The handmaiden did as she was asked with a sigh of exhaustion.

"Young lady, I hardly think the Baron would want you bringing trash into her chambers."

Another servant pulled a dress over the Heir's head and began braiding her hair hastily.

"It's not trash. It's my lucky stone. I need it."

The Heir snatched the stone off the countertop and rubbed the smooth side with her thumb. She'd gotten into that habit anytime she was going to visit the Baron. Or anytime she was nervous at all, really.

"What does she want, anyway? We shouldn't be meeting for another moon at least."

"What does who want, young Heir?" Lydia, one of the Heir's tutors, spoke up for the first time. The Heir hadn't even seen her leaning in the corner, waiting.

"Sorry, Miss Lydia. What does *the Baron* want?" The Heir blushed at her mistake. She should know better than to speak casually about the Baron. Even if she was only in the presence of her own handmaidens.

"The Baron has the right to summon the Heir whenever she feels necessary . . . within reason. It's not at all unusual for the Heir and the Baron to meet on occasion outside of the usual ceremonies."

The Heir slid her stone into a pocket while her nails were quickly double-checked and offered an extra cleaning. "It's unusual for *us*."

Lydia approached the Heir and knelt down beside her. "You're not wrong about that, young Heir." Lydia smiled at the Heir. She didn't have family here in the castle, not really. But the Heir had grown fond of Lydia. "You'll do swimmingly, blessed child. Listen to what the Baron has to say and do not speak out of turn. You are sure to learn something from this visit."

Lydia accompanied the Heir to the foot of the stairs leading up to the Baron's tower before letting go of her hand. "You know the way from here, young Heir."

The Heir slipped her hand into her pocket and began rubbing the stone. She had found it on a trip to the docks a few years earlier. When she asked why it was so smooth compared to most rocks, Lydia had explained that years of the waves crashing into it over and over again would eventually smooth out even the roughest surfaces.

The Heir took the first step up toward the Baron's chambers and looked back at Lydia. Maybe she could get out of the visit by feigning a stomachache. It wouldn't even really be pretending. Her stomach was in knots at the thought of sitting face-to-face with Baron Tamiyo, and her rubbing stone wasn't helping the way it usually did. She began to open her mouth, but Lydia cut her off before she could get a word out.

"Up you go, young Heir. You shouldn't keep Baron Tamiyo waiting any longer."

She turned around in defeat and began climbing.

Chapter 46

Beth

The winds howl against these towers. As if the oceans knew their crimes and wished to knock them into the sea.

—From the journal of Aphra of Alpha, Colonel of the Truthkeepers

Beth was on her knees, just a few lengths away from the crash site. Her vision was blurry, but as it started to refocus, she took in her surroundings. The God Rock had torn through the landscape and created a trench in the ground. She remembered following that with . . . Portia. *Where was Portia?*

She looked around, but the quick turning of her head made her dizzy all over again. Her head was spinning. She could hear voices nearby, but she could barely make them out. They didn't sound like Portia . . .

Her vision started to tunnel in, and the sound of her own heart beating thundered over everything else.

With eyes closed, she pictured Portia's hand in her own. *Breathe in. Breathe out. Slowly. Steady.* She tried to hear Portia's words in her ears and make the imagined whispers louder than the pounding in her head or her chest. After a few moments, her heartbeat slowed back down. She dared to open her eyes and, though her vision was still blurry, it wasn't tunneling any longer.

Slowly this time, Beth tried to look around. The first thing she noticed was one person kneeling down near the crash site. As her vision began to come into focus, she recognized the hulking figure. The templar from the swamp. Templar Malcolm. He was alone at the crash site and seemed to be moving pieces of the God Rock from its small crater into a large bag by his feet.

Without thinking, Beth tried to stand up and get closer. She knew she couldn't overpower the templar, but she just wanted to *see*. What was he doing up there? Before she could get to her feet, a hand gripped her shoulder and shoved her back down to the ground.

"Templar Malcolm. They're stirring." It was that same cocky recruit with the pretty face and square jaw from the swamp.

Beth lay on her back and shielded her eyes from the sun as she looked up at the recruit. "Radcliffe, right? Didn't expect to be running into you again so quickly. Did I miss anything exciting while I was out?"

"You know. Saw some pretty hills. Followed a trail of smoke. Snuck up and knocked you out before you placed your hands on the divine gifts of the God Stripe. So nothing too exciting." She could see the look of pride in his eyes as she stared up at him. He really thought he was doing some holy work here.

"How's your head?" Portia's voice came from the ground somewhere behind Radcliffe. Beth still found herself too woozy to actually sit up, but it was a relief to hear her voice.

"I feel like I fell out of a tree, fought a series of swamp beasts, and then got knocked out by some striping templars." Beth closed her eyes again and laid her head back on the ground to think. Was there any way out of this?

"Templar recruit. Don't give the kids too much credit," Portia shot back.

"Come one, show some respect, scavenger. Have you no shame?" Recruit Metz was standing guard over Portia.

Radcliffe laughed off Portia's insult anyway. "I have the Baron's word I'll become a templar the moment we finish this mission successfully. You can count on my ascension before the next full moon. There's a Sword of Power waiting for me in the weapons cache. Maybe the Baron's first request of Templar Radcliffe will be to use it to send you to your judgment."

Templar Malcolm shouted back from the impact site. "Enough chatter, sproutlings. Keep them quiet. Keep them where they are. We're almost through here."

Beth made her way back up to her knees and was able to see Portia on the ground below Metz. It looked like she may have taken a bit of a beating as well, but she didn't appear to be as hazy as Beth. Radcliffe looked ahead toward Templar Malcolm and seemed to be straining his eyes.

"Want to get in for a closer look?" Beth asked quietly enough that Malcolm wouldn't hear her.

"The God Rock is meant for the Baron's eyes. Only her chosen templar has the honor of preparing it for her."

Beth shrugged. "Seems kind of unfair to me. Templar Malcolm isn't the one who had to fight off a swamp beast. Why should he be the only one who gets to see it?"

Radcliffe knelt down to reach eye level with Beth. "I told you, I'll be a templar when I get back. I don't striping care what's in that crater. I just want to get back to Delta and claim my sword . . . and maybe be around to watch when Baron Tamiyo chucks the pair of you into the depths."

The hair on Beth's arm stood up straight as she felt a sudden drop in the temperature. She took a deep breath in and could smell a storm forming—one of the most dangerous parts of living out over the oceans were the water cyclones. Beth knew they were too distant from the ocean for that type of storm to reach them here, but something in the air felt the same. Her ears popped, and she saw Radcliffe look up to the sky to study the dark clouds swirling overhead.

"Uh, B? Are you seeing this?" Portia pointed behind Beth and up to the skies. Beth turned her head back toward Templar Malcolm and in the distance behind him saw a massive cyclone of dust and wind crashing down from the clouds. It was spinning wildly toward their plateau. It wasn't made of water, but it looked just as deadly.

Chapter 47

The Heir

To be nameless isn't always a bad thing. I was nameless myself for three decades, you know.

—Handmaiden's transcript of recurring conflict resolution meetings between Baron Agrius and the Heir

A guard with a big belly and a friendly face pushed open the heavy door outside Baron Tamiyo's chambers as the Heir reached the top of the twisting staircase. She nodded to him in appreciation as she walked past and entered the room with her head bowed.

The door creaked shut behind her. Just as she had been trained to do, she waited patiently for orders from the Baron while staring at the ground and rubbing the stone in her pocket. Rubbing the stone wasn't a part of the lesson. She had added that bit on her own. Nearly a full minute went by in silence before she heard the Baron let out an annoyed sigh.

"Must I remind you every time?" Tamiyo asked from

across the room, where she stood staring out one of the tower's windows. "You don't need to bother with those ridiculous rituals in my chambers."

"I apologize, my lady. My only intention is to offer you the respect and loyalty you deserve." She blurted out the memorized apology as she had been trained to do after she explained to her tutors that Baron Tamiyo didn't appreciate the traditions that she had been drilled on since she learned to speak.

Tamiyo chuckled. "Lydia's words sound just a bit forced coming out of your mouth, my child." Tamiyo turned to face the Heir and sat on the ledge of her window. "But I haven't summoned you here to debate the antiquated traditions we're forced to deal with."

Tamiyo gestured toward a seat across from her, and the Heir crossed the room and joined her.

"Why have you summoned me here then, my lady?" the Heir found herself asking. It was not good form to question the Baron, but Tamiyo had never been one to enforce those sorts of rules on the Heir and she truly was curious.

"I'm not sure, to be honest with you, child. I've sent my two closest friends off on an incredibly dangerous mission. I'm running out of people I can trust and I . . . well, I suppose I didn't want to be left alone with my striping thoughts any longer."

The Heir shifted uncomfortably at the use of inappropriate language. She didn't know what it meant exactly, but she knew it was *not* something she was supposed to say or hear. She found herself hoping that the Baron was not angry.

"I'm happy to keep you company, my lady." The Heir wasn't sure if she liked this more or less than the formal visits she was more accustomed to. The unpredictability still left her stomach in knots, but she did enjoy the idea of being someone Tamiyo could turn to. They had never been close, and she knew they were not supposed to become close, but she did long for friendship. Her handmaidens were kind, but they weren't really friends.

The Baron turned back to the window and looked out. Over her shoulder, the Heir could see that the view faced the other three islands and the mainland in the distance. The Heir found herself wondering how much dirt there might be on the mainland. And what sort of bugs she'd find if she ever got a chance to dig through it.

"Tell me, my Heir, have you chosen a name?" Tamiyo asked.

The Heir's breath caught in her throat, and her hand froze on her stone. Was this an accusation? Her voice hadn't seemed harsh, but the question wouldn't be asked lightly.

"Baron Tamiyo, my name will be selected on the day of my ascension ceremony. I wouldn't dare try to claim an identity while you still served the God Stripe."

Tamiyo smiled back.

"I've told you before, you don't need to be so formal with me. I'm not speaking to you as the Baron, just as . . . a friend." The Heir may be young and inexperienced, but she was certain an Heir and a Baron were not *friends*. No matter how much she might wish they could be. "I remember what it was like to be the Heir. It wasn't all that long ago, you know?" The Baron smiled at the Heir again.

"I know, my lady. You're still very young. I have much to learn from watching you rule before my own identity emerges."

The flattery seemed to roll right off the Baron. "When I was a girl I had decided on my identity by my sixth year in the training. The story of Tamiyo was one of my favorites. I used to ask my handmaidens to read it to me every night before bed. Do you know it?"

The Heir smiled. "Of course, my lady. I'm sure after you became Baron everyone learned the story."

The Baron nodded and picked up a treat from a nearby plate. She offered one to the Heir, who politely declined the food as she'd been trained to do. "You know, not everyone sees her as a hero. Handmaidens use her story to warn young children against rebelling from the rules. Ridiculous." She tossed the small treat into her mouth and threw her hands up in the air.

The pair smiled together this time.

"I've seen you out in the gardens, you know? Playing in the dirt, chasing the bugs around. Skipping your lessons." Tamiyo poked at the Heir playfully.

"I . . . I try not to miss my lessons, my lady. I do love to be outdoors, though. Especially near the plants."

"You know what you like, and you go along with the rest just enough to keep everyone unaware of your harmless passions. I admire it. I did the same when I was your age." The Heir didn't understand why, but she thought Tamiyo looked sad as she spoke about her own youth.

The Heir knew she wasn't supposed to question the Baron. "Did you love the gardens too, my lady?"

Tamiyo frowned. "It wasn't the soil for me, no. I mostly loved finding ways to irritate Baron Agruis."

Chapter 48

Malcolm

Serve the Oaths, no matter where they may take you.

—Proverbs of Templar Amaryte

None of Malcolm's trips to the mainland had prepared him for the disaster that struck the plateau. He could fight wyverns, he could navigate the swamps, and he could handle whatever he found at a crash site; but there was no outfighting or outsmarting a Land God's storm.

Older templars had warned him about land storms, and he'd heard horror stories about them in his boyhood. The Land God objected to humans walking on the dry land. The twisting cyclones of lightning were just another way these cursed places tried to swallow up any God Stripe-blessed creatures who dared to leave the Chain.

The swirling clouds seemed to come out of nowhere. Malcolm was looking at an enormous mass of dust and lightning within seconds. The wind tossed tree branches across the plateau and nearly blew him off his feet. A terrible gust of gust swept through the group and sent Metz soaring through the air.

"No!" Malcolm reached a hand out to catch Metz as the recruit was tossed across the plateau like a child's toy, but there was no hope. The winds swept him off the side and he was gone. Malcolm slammed a fist into the dirt and screamed in anger. The boy had trusted Malcolm with his life and this is what he had earned. A death on the cursed mainland, far from his family and the Chain. He would be lucky if they were able to secure his body to send him to the depths for judgement. Even that much wasn't guaranteed at this point. Another recruit that the old templar had failed.

The storm raged on around them. He needed to finish the mission. There was still the God Rock. No matter how many recruits died along the way, Tamiyo would forgive him once the bag was in her hands.

Malcolm knelt down and looked at the crater one last time to ensure he'd bundled all of the remaining debris. The mission was still a success. Now he needed to get the bundle back to Tamiyo without getting sucked into the swirling rage of the Land God.

He looked up again to check on the storm, which was racing toward his position at the crash site. Part of his mission was to destroy any remaining evidence of the God Rock's landing before heading back, but it seemed like the storm would be able to take care of the task for him. He reached down to pick up the bag and felt a tug at his waistline at the same time. At first he thought he was just losing his balance in the winds, but after a moment he realized what had really happened.

"Toss the bag over." He turned his back to the storm to find the curly-haired woman holding his own sword over her head and aimed at him. She may have no clue how to wield it, but swinging downward from overhead had the potential to slice him in two if she managed to connect.

Malcolm shouted over the sound of the storm. "That weapon was sent to me from the God Stripe! You've cursed yourself by touching it, heretic."

He looked over her shoulder and saw Radcliffe being wrestled to the ground by the other woman. Just when he was starting to trust the striping fool . . .

Malcolm wouldn't betray his Oaths and he certainly would never break his word to Baron Tamiyo. Not again. This bag would be delivered to her, or it would be destroyed. It couldn't fall into the hands of the heretics. His grip on the bag tightened as he looked over his shoulder to see how long he would have to wait before he could surrender to the storm and allow it to destroy the bag along with him.

Just as he turned to look for the swirls of lightning, he and his attacker were blown off their feet and back toward Radcliffe and the other woman. The vicious winds whipped at his face like the sting of jelly monsters from the depths as he crashed to the ground. He wrestled against the swirling elements and mustered all of his strength to hold his grip tight to the handle of the bag. Before he could reorient himself from the fall, he felt a powerful kick land squarely on his jaw. Pain ignited, and he reached for his mouth and nose by instinct, releasing the bag. He reached back out immediately, but it was too late. The wild winds blew the bag directly to the woman, as if the Land God wanted her to have it. As Malcolm fought back against the storm and tried to get up, she was already slinging the bag over her shoulder. Meanwhile her partner, who had somehow managed to keep hold of his weapon and not stab herself while soaring through the air, shoved a knee into his back and held the sword against the nape of his neck.

He began to shift the hidden weapon on his back forward by sliding the straps along his shoulder to pull the case towards the front of his torso. He froze in place as the heretic tightened her grip and pushed the sword into his neck hard enough to draw blood. She had to shout to make her words heard over the storm. "NOT ONE MOVE."

While he lay helplessly watching, he saw Radcliffe tackle the woman to the ground and rip the bag from her back. The recruit started to move toward Templar Malcolm to help free him, but he had to leap back when the storm hurled a large log toward him. The path of the swirling cyclone menacingly inched closer to the group, and Radcliffe continued backing up. The storm was on course to run straight between them.

This was the chance they needed. Malcolm had to trust that Radcliffe could carry out the mission from here. He would escape if he could; these two may be heretics, but they didn't seem like killers. If they were he would be dead by now. He was quite certain that if the storm didn't kill him, he'd have a chance to catch up to his recruit before long anyway.

He locked eyes with Radcliffe from across the God Rock's crater path and shouted. "TAKE IT TO HER. NOW! GO, BOY!"

The woman who Radcliffe had tackled to the ground sprung to her feet to charge at him but was cut off by the swirling storm before she could reach her target. The cyclone tore through the land, and she retreated back to the ground near Malcolm and her friend.

As the storm raged forward and the dust settled around them, there was no sign of Radcliffe. He had made it. He and the gifts from the God Rock were gone, and Malcolm would do everything he could to make sure these heretics never caught up to him.

Chapter 49

Beth

The gardens wilt on Delta. And the citizens of Alpha dance on the roofs of the stacks.

—From the journal of Aphra of Alpha, Colonel of the Truthkeepers

"*Striping* cursed storm. *Striping* stupid recruit. *Striping* ... Stripe!" Beth shouted the last one up into the sky. It seemed to be answered by a distant crack of thunder in the direction the storm had raged off toward.

Portia had bound the hulking templar's hands behind him and stripped him of every weapon she could find, but she still stayed in place with a knee in his back and the ancient Sword of Power held to his neck just for good measure. All he had left were the clothes he was wearing and an awkward case slung over his shoulders that seemed to be some type of storage device.

"What is this thing?" Portia asked as she smacked the rectangular case on his back.

"Ask the Gods on your judgment day, scum. You'll sooner get an answer from them than me." Malcolm replied through gritted teeth.

"If that's the way you want to do things, old man." Portia pulled the case off the beat up templar and flung it over her own shoulder. Beth was sure Portia would want to take a closer look at that when they had time, but at the moment, holding him in place seemed to be the priority. They were not planning to get caught by this man a third time.

"What the depths do we do now?" Beth shouted up at the clouds.

"You can submit to the Baron's mercy and turn yourselves in. Attempt to earn back some amount of favor with the God Stripe before your final judgment. Or you can build a hut and see how long you can survive out here before the Land God tears you to shreds."

"I don't think she was asking you," Portia advised.

"Come on, it's not a total loss. We can still get out of this. And we're not totally empty-handed." Portia nodded to the shining sword she was wielding.

"The Baron shows no mercy. They've seen us. We'd have to be in hiding for the rest of our lives. And that artifact? There's such a thing as priceless, and you're holding it. We could never move it. It's too forbidden. Even for our kind of customers." Beth was still walking circles around the crash site and thinking.

"He's right, you know? We might as well stay out here. The islands are never going to be safe for us again. I've ruined everything. What can we do? Kill a templar? Catch up to that recruit and get him out of the way before he can tell anyone who else was out here? I'm . . . I'm not going to make killers out of us. We're not her. We're not him." Beth looked down at the templar as she thought back to the day she lost her mother.

"We . . . we just need to slow down and think. There's got to be something else we can do. Some other angle." Portia said.

The bound templar on the ground joined the conversation uninvited yet again. "Listen. We need to leave this place. Let's start marching back toward the swamps, and you can plot your next inevitably ingenious move there. We're too far inland. The Land God won't have patience for us much longer."

Beth stopped her stomping and looked to Templar Malcolm. "What are you talking about?"

"You think that cursed storm is all the mainland has in store for us? We're not meant to walk these lands. Every second we overstay our welcome, the Land God's anger grows. We need to leave. *All* of us. Now.

Beth looked to Portia. She was onto him too.

Portia leaned down toward the old templar's ear. "What don't you want us to find out here?"

Templar Malcolm sighed in frustration. "There is no treasure here for you, scrapper. Nothing to steal and sell to the other bottom-island scum. This is cursed land, and it will bring you nothing but death. The next storm will be here any moment, and it will be far less forgiving than the last."

"Keep him down," Beth said. Portia continued holding Malcolm down while Beth increased the radius of her pacing. Why did he want them off this plateau so badly? There wasn't much to it, really. It was impressive to look at from a distance, but up close it was all just grass, dirt, and flat land. Flat land . . .

Beth strayed from her loop and jogged over toward the edge of the plateau. She looked out onto the rolling plains and admired the landscape. She spoke her next words quietly to herself, "Why is it so flat up here?"

Everything else is a rolling hill, she found herself thinking as she began walking the large loop around the outer edge of the plateau. But aside from some rocks and a bit of tall grass here and there, the surface of the plateau seemed to be perfectly flat. Was that normal? It wasn't like the rocky surfaces of the Chain, she knew that much. But something about it felt too perfect. Like it had been designed.

Her walk led her around the outside of the plateau, and she found herself thinking about how perfectly round the structure was in addition to its flatness. Nature could certainly produce perfect shapes. She'd seen gorgeous Depth shells that looked like art. It didn't seem impossible that a perfectly round and perfectly flat plateau could've formed out here, but it did feel . . . off somehow.

Beth completed her loop around the plateau and was back on the side near Portia and Malcolm again. She looked to the templar, who was watching her intensely. "Sure you don't just want to tell me what the stripe this thing really is?" She stared at Malcolm and waited for a response that didn't come. "Fine, then. I can figure it out for myself."

Beth walked over to Portia and gave her shoulder a squeeze as she reached for Templar Malcolm's belt and stripped it of his sidearm dagger. She returned to the outer rim of the plateau, dropped to her hands and knees, and began digging.

Chapter 50

The Heir

Look to the God Stripe, child. All the answers are there.

—Handmaiden's transcript of recurring conflict resolution
meetings between Baron Agrius and the Heir

Neither the Heir's training nor her past interactions with the Baron had prepared her for this sort of conversation. She stared out the window over the Baron's shoulder and daydreamed about returning to the gardens. The conversation wasn't unpleasant by any stretch, it was just . . . confusing.

Baron Tamiyo had never really shown any fondness for the Heir during their prior meetings. Now, seemingly out of the blue, she was here offering sweets and chatting about her childhood. The Baron and the Heir were only allowed to be left alone together for limited amounts of time, so the Heir just had to get through a few more minutes before an adviser and handmaiden would enter the room to conclude the visit. She could do this. And then she'd spend the whole rest of the day out there in the dirt.

"I find myself short of people I can trust on Delta today, my Heir." She huffed a dismissive and annoyed breath at the formality of the title. "I do wish you would just give me a name to call you, child."

"I'm sorry, my lady."

"Anyway, like I was saying, my dearest companions are away from the island. I'm running dangerously low on nearby friends, and I've grown sick of stressing about this God Rock myself. I need a friend, young Heir. Someone to distract me. That's all."

The God Rock . . . the Heir had seen it come crashing down from the heavens. She dreamed of someday being delivered the God Rock's messages herself. She shouldn't pry, but her curious mind started spinning with excitement and speculation.

"I'm sorry about your trusted allies, my lady. Are they . . . with the God Rock?" She tried to ask the question casually. As if she were just commenting on the tides.

Tamiyo pointed out the window and over the other islands, all the way out to the blurry mainland in the distance. "They're out there, yes. Securing the crash site, as is tradition. But I have concerns."

"It's as dangerous as they say, then? The mainland?" For the first time, the Heir didn't want their escorts to arrive at the room. It occurred to her just how much firsthand knowledge Baron Tamiyo might be willing to share that her tutors would consider frivolous and non-essential to her studies. "Is there soil there too, my lady?"

The Baron seemed almost confused by the question. "I . . . I've never been to the mainland myself, but yes, it is my understanding that travelers who survive the trek through the swampland have emerged on a cursed land full of storms and enormous beasts. That said, I do believe those cursed lands are green, which means there must be much more of that dirt you're so fond of."

The Heir tried to picture what it would be like to visit such a place. She had never really fantasized about which rules she would change when she became the Baron herself. But now, sitting here talking to Tamiyo, she found herself thinking about how hard it might be to change the rules so that the Baron could make a trip to the mainland when it was her time. She wanted to see those rolling green fields with her own eyes.

Chapter 51

Sly

If they come for us? After years of hiding away in the sea? We'll be prepared. Just as we've always been.

—The case of *Moira Vex v. The Council of War*, in retort

Sly and her new companions had made good time through the rest of the swamps and avoided run-ins with any other creatures. They broke through the forest line and into the rolling plains just in time to see Radcliffe sprinting across the massive field toward them.

Jonah and his two borrowed recruits raised their weapons in reflex at the approaching figure. Radcliffe slowed to a stop and realized how exposed he was in the wide-open field. Sly reached up to Jonah's raised sword and placed a hand on his forearm to gently lower his weapon. "It's okay . . . I know this fool."

She stepped forward through the group and made eye

contact with Radcliffe as she waved him forward. "Come on, Cliffe. It's reinforcements."

Sly could see Radcliffe breathe a sigh of relief from afar before he began sprinting toward them again.

Jonah stepped forward and stood next to Sly. "Can't help but notice he's alone, recruit." Sly had noticed, as well. She also noticed Jonah had yet to sheath his sword.

Radcliffe arrived and immediately took a knee to catch his breath. "What the stripe happened, Sly? Your striping prisoners are out there at the crash site!," he gestured back across the rolling fields, "I barely got away. Templar Malcolm is still with them."

"The God Rock, boy. Is it secure? Does Malcolm have it?" Jonah took a knee next to Radcliffe so they were eye to eye.

Radcliffe looked up at Sly for a moment. She could see he was still trying to figure out whether or not he should trust these new faces. She nodded to him.

"They saved my life, Cliffe. You can trust them."

He looked from Sly to the other recruits and back to Jonah before clutching the bag wrapped around his torso. "I have the God Rock. But Templar Malcolm, he needs help out there. The storm and the heretics—"

He was cut off by Jonah spinning around behind him and loosening the ties on the bag.

"Hey! The bag is my charge. What do you think—"

Jonah was apparently satisfied with whatever he saw, because he quickly resealed the bag and helped lift Radcliffe to his feet.

"You did well getting the God Rock away from danger. The Baron will recognize your efforts here, recruit."

Sly eyed the pack slung around Radcliffe. After all this time, it was right here. An arm's length away.

"Assuming we can make it back through there alive," Simone gestured into the swamps.

"And Templar Malcolm?" Radcliffe asked.

This time it was Jonah's turn to look back out over the open fields. "The God Rock is the primary objective. We need to get it back to Baron Tamiyo before anything else goes wrong out here."

Sly looked back at Jonah in disgust. "You're just going to leave him out there? He needs our help."

"Templar Malcolm has survived more trips to the mainland than any other living templar. He will find his way back to the islands. We have our mission." He still didn't take his eyes off the rolling plains and the stormy clouds moving overhead.

"No thanks to you," Sly mumbled to herself.

"He made me leave him on the plateau. There were two heretics there holding him down and a cyclone raging around. He was . . . I mean, they had the upper hand when I left." Radcliffe didn't look hopeful.

Sly stepped up next to Jonah and spoke softly. "We can get the God Rock back to the boats, but someone has to go back for him. The Oaths . . . he would never leave one of us out here like this."

She wasn't really sure if that was even true. Based on the stories she'd heard about Templar Malcolm's last batch of recruits, he didn't have the best record of making it home with everyone in one piece.

Jonah's eyes had left the rolling plains and were locked on to his sword once again. Sly saw the way his focus had changed at the mention of the Oaths.

"Templar Malcolm is strong. He's still alive up there." Sly nodded toward the massive round plateau in the distance that Cliffe had pointed back to. "But he needs a templar to make it back home."

Jonah's grip on his sword tightened, and he thrust it back into its sheath. He'd made up his mind.

"Simone, Arin—help Sly and Radcliffe get the bag back through the swamps and onto a boat. Don't stop until you're standing in front of Baron Tamiyo."

Arin and Simone looked at each other and seemed to beam with pride for the old retired templar. Maybe there was still hope for him after all.

"Yes, Templar," they replied in unison.

Jonah took his eyes off his sword hilt and looked at the bunch of recruits. "I need you to swear an Oath as if you were swearing it to the Baron and the God Stripe itself." The four of them looked to the adviser in anticipation. How much more could possibly be asked of them? "Don't dare to open that satchel. Not in the swamps, not on the boat, and not even once you are back on Delta. Hand it to the Baron herself and absolutely no one else. That bag is the voice of the God Stripe and meant for the Baron's eyes and ears only. Anyone else who bears witness to it will know the wrath of the God Stripe and the depths. None of you could survive looking into the face of the God Stripe."

"I swear it," the group of recruits all confirmed with no hesitation.

"Good. Then go now. You should be able to make it through the swamps before night falls again. Stay out of the waters and keep an eye toward the branches for any other wyverns."

Radcliffe looked to Sly at the mention of the flying beasts. She held up her arm to show the scratches where the massive talons had clamped hers.

"Remember your Oaths. Honor each other. Honor the Baron. Honor the God Stripe."

Jonah turned around and began jogging out over the open plains toward the plateau. *Good*, Sly found herself thinking. *What comes next will be much easier without an armed templar around to stop her.*

Chapter 52

Beth

I miss her some nights, despite her treachery. Our time together was so short before it all fell to pieces.

—From the journal of Aphra of Alpha, Colonel of the Truthkeepers

The foot-long dagger wasn't the best tool for digging, but it would do the trick in a pinch, and Beth didn't exactly have a shovel anywhere nearby.

"We're running out of time, scavenger. I'm warning you. We all need to go. NOW," Malcolm shouted.

Beth had been digging around in different spots on the plateau for nearly an hour. She wasn't sure exactly what she was looking for, but she knew she would know once she saw it. It was while digging her sixth hole that she struck the dagger down and heard the out-of-place sound of metal crashing into metal. The sound echoed across the plateau, and she looked up to see Malcolm's reaction. To her surprise, he looked completely shocked.

"What . . . What is that?" he asked from the ground.

"Let's find out," Beth replied as she began using her hands to wipe the dirt and patches of grass clear from the top of whatever she had dug up. She found herself wondering how she would be able to lug it back to the island if it was a massive haul of scraps or some other heavy treasure she could barter with.

As she cleared the debris off, a beat-up sheet of metal began to take form in the ground. It was similar to the scraps of sea debris the stacks were built out of, but more hardy and sturdy—a lot like the stuff Templar Malcolm's Sword of Power must have been forged with in the ancient days when the templar blades were all made. Beth had never bought the story about them being delivered from the God Stripe. They were weapons, just like the coral spears bandits on Beta used. Theirs just happened to be shiny and much sharper. Could she use whatever this was to make her own swords or daggers? She may not be able to sell an actual Sword of Power stolen from a templar, but make and distribute their own? That could work . . .

"B? What is it?" Portia called out.

"Some kind of . . . material. I don't know. It's massive. I can't get it free quite yet."

She cleared more patches of soil as she tried to find an edge or corner of the material. It seemed to have no end. How the depths was she supposed to dig up this hunk of trash?

As she cleared another patch of dirt, she found an extension coming off the metal. She dug around the area a bit more and cleared away what appeared to be a latch of some sort.

"What the . . ."

"What is it?!" Portia was losing her mind being stuck

holding Malcolm down instead of over there looking with Beth.

"Whatever you found . . . no good is going to come from it." Malcolm sounded defeated, but tried to issue one last warning anyway.

"I think . . . it's a door."

"A door? What are you talking about?" Portia took her knee off Malcolm's back. "Stay on your hands and knees." She ushered him forward as he crawled toward Beth, who was still just staring at whatever she had excavated.

"It says something on it, but I can't read whatever these markings are. Malcolm, what the stripe is a man-made door doing out here in the middle of the striping mainland? What aren't you telling us?" Beth looked to the templar for answers, but she didn't really believe he'd actually offer any.

"I truly don't know. I just know this place is cursed and we're in danger as long as we stay here." Malcolm said as he and Portia got close enough to see the door in the ground. Portia pushed him back down to his belly.

"This doesn't make any sense. Nobody lives out here. Nobody's ever lived out here. Who could've built that? The Gods?" Portia was grasping at straws.

Beth knocked on the door and waited a few moments. "I don't think anyone's home."

"I striping hope not," Portia blurted out.

"Let's see what's inside," Beth suggested with a grin.

"That's what we're here for, right?" Portia agreed.

Chapter 53

Sly

I'm not foolish enough to hope for never ending peace. But we can be vigilant without sacrificing our children.

—The case of *Moira Vex v. The Council of War*, closing statements

The group had started off with Radcliffe in the lead, followed by Arin, Sly, and then Simone at the tail. Radcliffe turned around and realized he had somehow gotten separated from the rest of the party. He had heard the steady footsteps behind his own just moments ago, so they couldn't be far.

He pulled the bag's strap tighter around his torso, concentrating on the weight of the God Rock debris on his back, and waited for a few moments. They would catch up to him. He must've just been going too fast. He took a step back in the direction he had just come from and listened to the sounds of the swamps. Blood flies buzzed overhead, lizards scurried across the ground, but there were no footsteps.

He would have to go on without them. Traveling through the swamps alone was dangerous, and he didn't like the idea of leaving the other recruits out here to get lost, but he was the one Templar Malcolm entrusted with the God Rock. He had to get it back to Baron Tamiyo as quickly as he could. Radcliffe quietly spun around and nearly screamed when he found Sly standing in front of him.

"For stripe's sake, Sly! How the depths did you get ahead of me? Where are the others?" Radcliffe whispered to her. He wasn't sure why, but he felt like they were in danger.

"How did you fall so far behind!" she replied back in a hushed tone. "We're right through here, come on."

Sly stood to the side to leave space for Radcliffe to pass through the clearing she had just pointed to. When he saw Arin and Simone unconscious and bound on the ground in the small clearing, his hand raced to the hilt of his weapon, but it was too late. The world went dark for Radcliffe as Sly rammed her polearm into the back of his head.

She wasn't sure why, but she checked to make sure he was still breathing as she knelt down to remove the bag from his torso. She wasn't here to hurt him. She wasn't here to hurt anyone, really. But that bag was never going to get to the Baron if she could help it.

She propped Radcliffe up against a log near Arin and Simone. They would all wake up before long. As long as they stirred before a wyvern or lizard found them, they should still be able to escape with their lives. She didn't want to hurt them, but she'd do whatever she needed to in order to complete her mission.

Sly slung the bag over her own shoulder and pulled the straps tight. She was nearly done now. Just a little farther to go, and then this would all be over. She would be going home and she'd never have to step foot on those cursed islands again.

Chapter 54

Malcolm

It is not our place to question the order when the Baron speaks, only to swing the sword.

—Proverbs of Templar Amaryte

Malcolm heard them coming while the scavengers were staring into the hatch they had just flung open. At first, he suspected it was reinforcements. It felt like it'd been ages since he sent up the purple smoke. Tamiyo must've sent another team to offer assistance, and they should be here by now.

But this didn't sound like a templar and their recruits.

"It's black as the depths in there. Light a torch, will you?" The woman who'd dug her way into the hole was sticking her head in there blindly. The other one knelt down, still with a knee in Malcolm's back, and started fumbling through a backpack.

Malcolm could've sworn he heard the sound of a small

pack of animals running across the plains below and stopping near the plateau. He didn't want to stick around to see who had been riding them.

He whispered in a harsh tone. "They're here. We have to go *now*. There's no time for this."

The girl pulled her head out of the dark hole in the ground and was grinning from ear to ear. "It's too late, old man. We're not leaving until we see what you've been hiding out here. And nobody is coming—"

She was cut off by the sound of metal clanging against rock, followed by a scraping sound. The three of them all looked toward the edge of the plateau, where a metal claw attached to a thick length of rope was dragging along the surface, looking for something to catch on to. The claw missed any holds and dropped off the side, but not before two others were thrown up to the plateau surface and landed on either side of the original one.

Beth turned back to Malcolm, who began trying to scramble and make his way free from Portia's grip. "Who in the depths is climbing up here, Templar?"

"Stop moving or I'm going to accidentally cut you!" Portia pleaded with Malcolm in a hushed tone. He didn't care. He'd rather have some blood on his neck than be here when whoever that was arrived.

"Someone who is an enemy to both of us," he replied.

Malcolm bucked up and managed to toss Portia off his back. She landed nearby with his sword in one hand and a lit torch in the other.

The old templar began to run toward another portion of the plateau border, away from the rope claws and the growing sound of climbing, but a few strides into his jog he saw yet another pair of the claws swing up to the plateau landing. There was no escaping. They were too close to get away now. He could hear each step they took as they scaled the plateau wall.

The two scavengers seemed to be frozen in place. They had no idea what was happening here. He spun around and raced back toward his captors. "Inside. Now!"

"So you do know what's down here. I knew it, you striping liar," said Beth.

Malcolm stood over the dark entryway into the ground and looked down into the black. "I don't. But I know it's got to be safer than staying out here with them." With that, he dropped into the darkness alone.

The heretics scooped up their things and followed.

Chapter 55

Beth

We lost a dozen Truthkeepers last night. These halls hold secrets and dangers we hadn't anticipated.

—From the journal of Aphra of Alpha, Colonel of the Truthkeepers

Beth's hands grasped the rungs of a ladder she could barely see as she descended into the ground. Portia carried the torch below her, but the flame didn't offer much light up where she was. She'd pulled the hatch mostly closed, but she didn't seal it. She found herself believing Malcolm. Whoever was coming was trouble, but she wasn't crazy about the idea of trapping herself down here either.

She waited at the top of the ladder and tried to listen to hear what was happening on the other side of the hatch. The door was thick, though, and it seemed to block out all sound from above.

"Beth . . ." Portia used her name in front of the templar.

Apparently she was giving up on escaping back to the islands and blending in. "What the hell is this?"

"Something none of us have a right to see, scavenger," Malcolm replied, even though the question wasn't directed at him.

Beth climbed the rest of the way down the ladder, which felt as tall as three stories of homes back in the stacks, and eventually landed with solid ground beneath her feet. The enormous chamber was devoid of light outside of the reach of Portia's torch. Beth could see Portia's outline and the large templar standing next to her. His hands were still bound, but that didn't mean he wasn't dangerous. For the moment, he didn't seem to be causing any trouble.

Beth pulled an unlit torch out of her bag as she walked toward them. They were staring at the wall, but Beth's mind couldn't really process what she was seeing even as she got close enough to stand shoulder to shoulder with Portia.

"What . . . what are these?" Beth reached out and ran her hands along the wall, which was covered in massive, colorful tubes. She looked up and confirmed the wall was covered in similar pipes or ropes or whatever they were as high as she could see. The whole wall also seemed to curve slightly outward. She suspected it followed the shape of the round plateau they were standing inside of.

"They're man-made for sure," Portia said as she kneeled down and ran her hands along the tubes. Some were as thick as a human leg, and others were thinner than fingers and clumped together in strands. "This whole place is man-made."

"None of that matters. We should move. They're sure to see the hatch up there now," Malcolm warned. He was the only one looking back toward the ladder in fear. Beth and Portia were too busy trying to figure out the purpose of the mysterious place.

Portia pushed some of the more flexible colorful tubes aside and ran her hands along the wall. "I know what this is."

Beth joined her and began examining the wall, as well. She looked at Portia and grinned as the revelation hit her. "Sea bones?"

"Sea bones." Portia agreed. "Far bigger and less damaged than the ones that built our stacks, but this is the same material. Someone built this whole striping place out of massive sea bones."

Beth leaned her torch against Portia's to light it and then jogged across the corridor in the opposite direction. She covered about twenty lengths before finding a wall that stood opposite the first one. It was also rounded and covered in a mess of tubes that she couldn't wrap her head around.

Portia and Malcolm walked over and joined her.

"Not very wide," Portia noted and then held her torch out into the darkness that ran down the middle of the room. "But I bet it goes all the way around the plateau. Like a giant loop."

"Why, though?" Beth wondered aloud.

Portia smiled. "Remember when we were kids and we used to talk about a secret way to get from island to island?" They began walking along the enormous corridor.

"We said we'd dig a hole down through the base of Beta. And then build a hallway underneath that went to Charlie. And another on the other side to Alpha." Beth remembered it. They had always been scheming. The schemes just got more realistic as they grew older. No more saddle designs for wyverns or impossible hallways connecting islands together.

"Right. Like a bridge, but underground. I think that's what this is."

Malcolm scoffed. "But your imaginary hallways had a purpose. To connect the islands in a new way. To sneak under the noses of the bridge guards. What does this connect to?"

Beth had no idea, and from the look on her face, Portia didn't either. The enormous hallway they were walking down did seem to be a long slow turn, which would likely eventually lead all the way back to where they started. So why build a massive secret hallway if it was just a circle and didn't go anywhere? Beth wasn't sure, but she suspected it had something to do with those tubes on the wall.

"Maybe there's more in the middle somewhere? Or farther below? Just keep an eye out for other doors or hatches."

"So, while we're looking . . . why don't you tell us what you know, Malcolm? I think we're a little too far along to keep up the secrets at this point," Portia prodded.

Malcolm walked along between the two of them and stayed in the torchlight. Beth noticed how frequently he looked back in the direction of the ladder. He really was terrified of something.

"I honestly had no idea this was down here. I—"

Beth laughed. "You're so full of it."

"Can you hold your tongue long enough for me to finish, bottom islander?"

She rolled her eyes, though nobody could see it down here. "Please, go on, Templar. Can't wait to hear what comes next."

Portia reached behind Malcolm and shoved Beth. "Let him finish. I think he's ready to tell the truth . . . or at least part of it."

"I only *know* part of it. That really is the truth. And that's the truth for everyone except for the Baron herself. She shares pieces of the secrets, yes, but nobody except the sitting Baron knows everything the God Stripe has to hide."

"So. Which parts of the great secrets *do* you know, then?" Beth asked as she bent down to examine the floor a bit closer.

"I know . . . I know there are gifts from the God Stripe," he began. Beth started to protest, but Portia hushed her. "Things that shouldn't exist. That there'd be no way for humans to create."

"Things like what? That sword of yours?" Portia asked.

"Yes. But more than the swords and the shields. Things you couldn't believe."

Beth gestured to the massive tube they were walking through. "You'd be surprised what I could believe at this point. Try me."

"Torches that don't require a flame. Medicines that cure diseases that should kill a person. Moving pictures that . . . that speak." Beth and Portia looked at each other in disbelief. "And things . . . things that remind me of this place. I truly didn't know it was here, but I feel the touch of the God Stripe in this cave."

Beth gestured up to the dark ceiling. "And the people up there? Who were you so scared of?"

Malcolm instinctively reached to his waist for his sword's hilt before remembering it wasn't there. "There are other people. *Cursed* people. Who . . . they live on the mainland."

"That's . . . That's not even possible. The storms, the creatures. Nobody can survive out here." Beth had obviously considered the possibility before, but everyone knew the mainland was uninhabitable. That's why they dealt with life on the lower islands. A crowded life in poverty on the bottom islands was better than no life at all.

"It shouldn't be possible. Like I said, they're cursed. Blessed by the evil God of the mainland. They usually stay out of our way and steer clear of the islands, but when a God Rock falls this far inland, they sometimes try to steal the word of God from our Baron." Beth could hear the disdain in Malcolm's voice. But there was fear there too.

"So you've run into them before then?" Portia asked.

"Not for many years, but yes. Early in Baron Tamiyo's

reign. Templar Mullen, Templar Jonah, a handful of recruits, and I were on a mission much like this one."

"Three templars? That's a lot of resources for one retrieval." Beth found herself believing Malcolm for some reason.

"God Rocks don't fall often, but when they do it's essential they are retrieved for the Baron as quickly as possible. In those days, there were more templars and more trust to go around," Malcolm explained. "We made it to the God Rock first, but we weren't fast enough. They caught up with us just inside the swamps and ambushed our squad. They shot down the recruits with arrows like they were nothing. Templar Mullen was carrying the package, but Jonah and I were taken prisoner. They wanted to know what the God Rock was. Why it was so important to us."

"How'd you get away?" Beth asked.

"They marched us out of the swamps and set up camp out here on the rolling plains. They tied us up and rested for the night, and I was sure we would be swept away by a cyclone before morning came. Jonah's bindings weren't tight enough, and he managed to slip out."

"So he cut you loose and you ran a cyclone was behind you?" Beth was engrossed in the story now. She didn't romanticize the templars the way children did, but she did want to learn as much about these mainlanders as she could.

"The coward ran. He tried to loosen my bindings, but he couldn't find anything sharp nearby. And when he thought he heard one of the guards stirring, he bolted. Left me for dead." Beth could hear how badly the betrayal had hurt Malcolm. Even all these years later, the bitterness and disappointment crept into his voice.

"Striping depths . . . that's brutal. How did you get away?" Beth asked as they continued walking the long circular path.

"I waited. Three days they dragged me across these plains. Questioning and torturing me along the way. I was certain I was a dead man. Doomed to die in the domain of the Land God and never ascend to the God Stripe. They gave me enough water to stay alive, but I was starving and losing strength fast."

"So, how'd you make it back?" Portia lifted her eyes up from the floor where she'd been searching for some secret door or hatch and looked at Malcolm. She felt like she was noticing all those scars on his face for the first time.

"On the third evening, a squad of real templars ambushed the group. Mullen, Zorra, and Rikor. Baron Tamiyo sent them for me. We were far enough inland and I was weak enough that the mainlanders had lowered their guard. They didn't bother covering their tracks, being quiet, or keeping a post awake at night. The templars came over the hill and cut down every last one of them. I barely remember the rest, to be honest with you. I'm pretty sure they carried me back across the plains and through the swamps on a stretcher."

"And Jonah? What happened with him?" Beth wondered aloud.

"Early retirement. The Baron had . . . other plans for him," Malcolm explained.

"The mainlanders . . . what did they want? Once the God Rock was long gone, why were they keeping you alive? Why drag you across the plains with them?" Portia asked the old templar.

"They questioned me for most of the first two days. What I knew about the Baron, about the mainland, about the God Rocks and the God Stripe. What was happening on the islands. I told them less than I've told you."

"And on the third day?" Portia asked.

"They . . . changed on the third day. They began talking about their way of life. Where we were going. What kind of lives the people there led. I think they were trying to beat me down until I was weak enough that they could earn my allegiance." Malcolm stopped as they arrived at another ladder. It looked identical to the one they had descended.

"No way we walked all the way around this thing already. Multiple entry points, I guess?" Beth suggested. "I'm going to head up and see where this one comes out."

"Are you striping mad?! Haven't you been listening to what I'm saying? They're up there. You could open that hatch right under their feet." Malcolm was terrified. Rehashing those three days of captivity had really done a number on him.

"Relax. I'll be careful and barely crack it open."

"B . . . just be really careful." Malcolm may have been terrified, but Portia's concern was a lot more convincing to Beth. They'd come too close to losing each other on this trip. This was no time to take unnecessary risks.

"I won't go if you don't want me to," Beth said to her.

"Good! We wait down here at least another hour. Maybe even until sunrise. Then we can head back for the swamps," Malcolm suggested.

"She was talking to me." Portia shook her head at Malcolm. "I want to know what they're up to. I think we should look."

Beth smirked. "It's a wide ladder. The three of us can climb up together."

Portia nudged Malcolm forward toward the ladder, and the three of them began to climb. They stopped at the top, and Portia gagged Malcolm. "Just in case it's actually a pack of your old templar buddies up there. You understand." The anger in his eyes suggested he did not.

Beth twisted the seal on the hatch and very slowly cracked the door open.

Chapter 56

The Heir

Do you not trust me, Heir? Or do you not trust the God Stripe?

—Handmaiden's transcript of recurring conflict resolution meetings between Baron Agrius and the Heir

There was a knock on the doors to Tamiyo's chambers, which the Heir knew would signify the end of their time alone together. Tamiyo looked to the door in disappointment.

"I suppose I'll be back to staring out the window on my own then, won't I?"

The Heir smiled at the Baron, with whom she was feeling much more comfortable now. "I'm sorry they limit our time together so strictly, my lady. I very much enjoyed your company. And I'm sure your friends will be back soon after a successful mission."

"Tell me, young Heir. Do you ever think of family?" Tamiyo asked.

The Heir gasped. They'd broken many rules in this exchange, but talk of family was strictly forbidden. The Heir was selected by the Baron and lived for one purpose. The short life she had as an infant before being claimed as an heir was erased from history once she was taken to Delta.

"It is forbidden. I live to serve only the God Stripe." The Heir fell back to her rote answers. She could never admit to wondering about her own parents. Her own island. Her own family.

"Of course, of course. I know it's strange, but for the longest time, I thought of your family when I tried to imagine my own." Tamiyo confided.

The Heir couldn't help her curiosity. "My family?"

"Well I have no memories of my own, of course. I tried to find them after my ascension, of course. As I'm sure nearly all Barons do who aren't ashamed of their natural curiosity. I tracked them down through Jonah's sources, but my parents were dead. It was too late."

"I'm terribly sorry. Ascended to the God Stripe, I'm sure. Being rewarded in the heavens for your divine service."

Tamiyo chuckled at the sincerity of the sentiment. "Perhaps, my darling nameless one. But, regardless, your family is the only family I'd ever seen. The only real family. The anger in your father's eyes as my gaze lingered on you and your mother. The tears that streaked your mother's face as I took you from her arms." Tamiyo pulled her dress up to her knee to reveal her calf. "The sting of your sister's bite as she tried to take down the Baron herself."

"My sister?" the Heir asked.

Tamiyo laughed again as she looked at the scar and ran a finger over it. "Well, the old you's sister. The Heir has no family, correct?"

The Heir imagined an older sister. One brave and angry

and foolish enough to attack the Baron. She desperately tried to search for the words. They'd already broken so many rules, how much further could she allow this to go?

"Assaulting the Baron is assaulting the God Stripe itself. Was my- Was *the child* punished?"

Tamiyo frowned as she lowered her dress back down over the old scar. "Templar Malcolm would've had her head if I didn't stop him. Though he wasn't Templar Malcolm yet, I suppose. Still just a recruit. He was so quick to soar to my side though. As if he believed a small child really could end me. Regardless, I admired her spirit, my Heir. She was a fighter. I wonder how much of that is in you. Her punishment was taken on by her mother. A final gift from a loving parent. And the first act of Malcolm's service after his quick ascension to full templar."

The Heir could imagine what that punishment must've looked like. Her birth mother was with the God Stripe now, no doubt.

"I don't know what to say, my Lady."

"Your sister defined my rule in many ways. I didn't set out to be cruel. To be strict. To hurt anyone . . . She defied me under the light of the God Stripe in front of her whole island. On my first day wearing the crown. What was I to do? She made the choice for me. She created Tamiyo the Cruel."

The Heir was stunned. She allowed herself the fantasy of exploring the islands someday. Perhaps even the mainland in search of larger gardens. But never lingered on the idea of her true parents. The God Stripe was her only family. She had no siblings. No mother willing to sacrifice herself in an act of love for her and her sister. She tried not to linger on the idea that Templar Malcolm had ended her mother's life. That was a dark path to dwell on and she pushed the image out of her mind, focusing on this idea of a fearsome sister instead.

"I'm sorry that you never got to see your family. Sorry that I'll never see mine either, I'm sure." The Heir said.

The Baron looked truly sad. The Heir had sensed the loneliness in her before. The anxiety. But the full weight of her sadness was rising to the surface. "It's what the God Stripe wills, I suppose."

"Your friends, though." The Heir looked towards the window and across the ocean to the mainland. "They're your family now. And they'll be back from their quest with your prize soon. I'm sure of it."

"I admire your optimism, child. I can't say I feel so sure. Something tells me there are problems out there. It may not be long before I have no friends left." Tamiyo stood from her chair and began tending to her hanging garden near the window.

"I am your friend, my lady." The Heir looked back to the door, where she knew her handmaiden was listening from the other side, and lowered her voice. She pushed away the thoughts of that broken family on Alpha. Of that life that she would never know. She was right where she belonged. "I am your family. And you can visit me down in the gardens whenever you need to see a friendly face." The Heir grabbed one last sweet off the tray as she headed for the door. "Do you know the tale of Templar Aphra, my lady?"

Tamiyo looked up from her plants. "I don't believe I do, my Heir."

"Ah. I think you would enjoy it. And when my time has come, I think everyone on the islands will know it." The Heir lowered her head and walked to the door as the second knock came.

"I hope to see you again soon, Lady Aphra," Tamiyo whispered through a smile as she looked back at her plants.

"That would be very lovely, Baron Tamiyo." The Heir

opened the door and left the tower to return to her gardens. She decided it would be best not to dwell on a sister who had bitten Baron Tamiyo and lived to fight another day. Instead, she would dream about the mainland. And reaching it for herself one day to see its soil for herself.

Chapter 57

Jonah

Baron Tamiyo made no shortage of enemies during her nameless era. You must quickly decide which advisers and handmaidens can be trusted. Purge the rest.

—Excerpt from the departure letter of Lord Drolt, Senior Adviser to Baron Agrius

The rolling plains were as beautiful as Jonah remembered them. Despite the way he'd left things on his last trip to the mainland, he did always miss these open fields. Of course the storms were terrifying, and he'd never forget what he did to Malcolm out here, but the view . . . even the top of Baron Tamiyo's tower didn't compare.

Young recruit Radcliffe had explained that Malcolm was last seen in distress on top of the plateau, and the massive landmark was certainly hard to miss. Jonah saw a few wind storms rolling by in the distance, but he seemed to have a clear path to his old friend for now.

If Malcolm had managed to get himself captured by the heretical scavengers as Radcliffe suggested, Jonah felt fairly certain he'd be able to help him escape. It wouldn't make up for leaving him out here all those years ago, but it was something. If Malcolm was still alive, Jonah would do whatever he could to protect him.

The real threat wasn't going to be the scavengers, though... it would be the mainlanders. After Malcolm was returned from captivity, he and Templar Mullen had petitioned Baron Tamiyo for a full-scale hunt of any remaining mainlanders. The pair understandably never wanted another templar to have to worry about that kind of assault while on an already dangerous mission, and their plan made sense. Jonah backed their petition, despite the fact Malcolm wouldn't even speak to him; but Baron Tamiyo ultimately denied the request. She explained that the God Stripe did not want them waging open war against the cursed mainlanders and their Land God. The islanders should conserve their resources and focus on protecting and advancing the Chain. If they were attacked on a mission, obviously, fighting back and taking whatever lives necessary was permitted, but there would be no hunt and no war. She confided in Jonah alone that there was a decades old truce keeping their islands safe from an all out assault by the mainlanders and she wouldn't be the one responsible for breaking it.

All these years later, Jonah still wasn't sure if he fully understood Baron Tamiyo's logic on the decision. The mainlanders were a serious threat and already a drain on resources. If they were not a problem, then the Depth Walkers wouldn't be charged with patrolling the waters so diligently. The decision was even more strange considering how close Baron Tamiyo and Malcolm had always been. If there was anyone who Tamiyo would be willing to start a war for, it seemed like it would've been Malcolm.

But her ruling stood despite months of appeals and heated arguments. The God Stripe had spoken, and her mind would not be changed.

As Jonah crested a hill on the plains, he set eyes on the plateau and scanned the horizon for any sign of the mainlanders. Knots in his stomach reminded him of the threat ahead. In that moment, he suddenly regretted that he had failed to convince the Baron to end the secret conflict by hunting down the remaining mainlanders all those years ago. He feared he was going to have to face them again before long, but this time there would be no army of templars by his side.

Chapter 58

Beth

Our occupation has taken ... a turn. The tower does not belong to us.

—From the journal of Aphra of Alpha, Colonel of the Truthkeepers

Beth nudged the hatch open a sliver and it let out a mechanical moan that echoed through the chamber below. The trio held their breaths in terror, waiting to see if the creaky door would give them away. After a moment frozen in silence without anyone ripping open the door the rest of the way, Beth pushed up on the hatch a little more, until it was open just enough that they could peer out at the surface of the plateau.

They'd walked farther than she imagined in the hidden hallway, but she was right about the direction they were heading. The corridor seemed to be looping them around the outside border of the plateau. She could see what little remained of the trail the God Rock had left back in the direction they came from. The storm had destroyed most of the path, unless you really knew what you were looking for. Standing over the former crash site was a group of people Beth had never seen before. The mainlanders.

The mainlanders didn't look as alien as Beth had expected, though she wasn't sure why she thought they would. They were just people. They had similar physiques to the islanders, but they seemed to be built a little thicker. There was more muscle and weight to them. They could've passed for templars if they were wearing the right armor and clothing. In their current state, they could never be mistaken for islanders, though. Their skin was far too light, for one, but their clothing was also unlike anything an islander would have ever seen. They dressed in layers and their wardrobe seemed to be covered in some kind of fur.

The group wasn't as big as Beth expected from the number of claws flung up onto the plateau surface. She counted ten people she could see from this angle. There was a clear ringleader, who the others seemed to look to for direction.

Beth stole a glance at Malcolm and saw the fear in his eyes. She pulled the gag down out of his mouth, now that she was feeling more certain he'd been honest with them about everything. "That them?" she asked, even though she already knew the answer.

"It's them," he whispered back through gritted teeth. "Scouring the crash site to see if we left anything behind. They won't find a trace."

Beth thought she heard some pride in his voice as he made that point. The old soldier felt like he had accomplished his mission, even though he was stuck here with them.

At that point, they heard the sound of someone else crawling up one of the hanging ropes. The group of mainlanders spun around and began to reach for weapons on their backs and in their belts. No coral spears or Swords of Power, but they seemed to have something to call upon if a fight was coming. The party carried long pointed sticks, quivers full of longbeak feathered arrows, and bows.

Beth, Portia, and Malcolm all looked to the plateau's edge where the group's weapons were pointing and waited to see who was walking into this trap. Beth immediately panicked at the thought of Malcolm seeing a rescue party climb over the edge and giving away their location to try and warn them.

She turned to him and whispered, "Not a peep, Malcolm. No matter who comes over that ledge. Or Portia puts your blade to good use, all right?"

He nodded, but she had her doubts.

After a long moment of suspense, a hand gripped the surface of the plateau, and a leg swung over the side. Beth didn't recognize the figure right away from the distance, but Malcolm's sigh of disappointment let her know he knew the climber.

"She's walking right into a trap . . . and with no backup? What is the depths is she doing here? They should be back at the boats by now."

Once she stood up and dusted herself off, Beth recognized Sly. She didn't fully understand how Sly wasn't being digested by a wyvern right now, but she breathed a sigh of relief at the realization that the recruit's death wasn't on her hands.

"Maybe she's looking for us?" Portia offered up quietly. "She must be a true candidate for templar ascension, huh? We didn't leave her in a great spot."

The group approached Sly, but it seemed like they were actually lowering their weapons rather than threatening her. Beth wondered if they were feeling safety in numbers against the single recruit.

"What's going on? Is she trying to bargain with them?" Malcolm wondered aloud.

"I can't hear very well," Beth replied, even though the question wasn't really directed at her. The woman who looked like the leader of the group reached out and embraced Sly in a hug while a handful of the others clapped her on the back. "But they definitely don't look upset to see her."

"What the stripe is going on here?" Malcolm's anger was bleeding through, and his voice was louder than Portia or Beth were comfortable with. Beth looked at the gag, but worried that trying to put it back in would cause more noise than just letting him be.

Portia rested a hand on his forearm. "Stay calm. We don't know what we're seeing."

But what they were seeing was pretty difficult to misinterpret in Beth's opinion. Sly knew these people. What that meant, she wasn't so sure about. Was the recruit somehow working with the mainlanders? How could that even be possible? The reality of the situation became inarguably clear when Sly began to unstrap a very familiar bag from her back and throw it down at the leader's feet.

"Oh, striping—" Beth started as the leader patted Sly on the shoulder and bent down to pick the bag up. Before she could finish her curse, Malcolm shouldered Portia to knock her off balance and used his bound hands to rip the carrying case away from her. He slung the case over his own shoulder and pushed his way to the top of the ladder despite Beth and Portia's attempts to hold him in place. The templar flung the hatch the rest of the way open and sprang out of their hiding spot. Beth was sure he was running headfirst to his death, and she immediately started searching for an exit route for her and Portia. She was tempted to pull the hatch shut and wait it out below, but there was no way the group had missed their heads poking out in shock as Malcolm charged out screaming, "TRAITOR!"

Portia looked down at the sword hanging from her belt. "He's unarmed..."

"And don't forget his hands are bound too," Beth added.

As he raced toward the group, they drew bows and aimed spears at the old templar. He reached for the strap that was slung around his chest and tugged on it to pull the long rectangular case from his back to his front where he could reach it. Apparently he hadn't shared all of his secrets with Beth and Portia, because he pressed his thumb to the top of the case and the latch swung open. They were right. It was some type of storage case, but they had no way to predict the sort of artifact that was stored inside.

Malcolm pulled a long, black weapon out of the case and aimed it at the mainlanders. They collectively stepped back in surprise, and even the bow-wielding members of the group seemed frightened of . . . whatever it was the old templar had pointed at them.

"What the depths is that thing?" Beth looked to Portia in puzzlement.

"I have no idea. But why didn't he pull it out on us if it's so scary?" Beth didn't know the answer to Portia's question either. All she knew was she didn't want to get back on the templar's bad side.

One of the mainlanders attempted to quickly draw his bow and take a shot at Malcolm, but before he had even pulled it tight, the templar had activated his weapon, and a crack echoed across the plateau as the bowman flew off his feet, landed on his back several lengths away, and began bleeding on the ground.

"God Stripe save us..." Portia muttered.

The rest of the mainlanders were frozen in place. Nobody

bent down to assist the bowman bleeding on the ground for fear the next shot may be aimed at them.

Malcolm leveled his weapon at Sly and stopped walking a few lengths away from the group. He wouldn't need to be any closer with that monstrosity he was carrying. "Care to explain what the stripe is going on here, recruit?"

Sly searched for words with her hands still frozen in the air. "I . . . I had my own mission. From the Baron."

The word *Baron* was barely out of her mouth before Malcolm had lowered the weapon to her feet and fired off a shot that made Sly jump into the air. She landed unharmed as Malcolm aimed the weapon upward back at her chest.

"That's the only warning shot you get, recruit. No. More. Lies." Malcolm had lost any remaining patience he had. "Nobody knows the Baron better than I do. And she doesn't trust anyone more than she trusts me. But I do believe you had your own mission. It just wasn't from the Baron, was it? You called that monster in the swamp a tentacler. Who taught you that word?"

Sly's eyes shifted toward the woman in the furs who seemed to be the leader of the group. She had long red hair that was tightly braided. Her pale face grew even lighter as she watched Malcolm's weapon focus on Sly.

"This one then?" Malcolm asked as she followed Sly's eyes to the woman. "How long? When did you betray our Oaths and our God?" He pointed to the God Stripe in the sky as he looked at her with disappointment.

Sly looked like she was too frightened to open her mouth again, and instead the woman in the furs spoke. "She was always ours, my friend. She was a born mainlander who was raised for this mission. We smuggled her onto the islands years ago."

This time it was Malcolm's face that drained of color. "That's . . . not possible. You want me to believe you smuggled a mainlander onto an upper island *years ago* and nobody ever noticed her?"

"Although it may be hard to believe, you don't know everything that comes on and off your beloved Chain, Templar."

Beth couldn't help but think the woman was right. She and Portia had been smuggling contraband from island to island since they were twelve years old. They'd even transferred scraps from the swamps back to the islands a handful of times. Would smuggling a person be just as easy? If they knew how to blend in, it didn't seem that far-fetched.

"Hand over the bag and the girl. I'll get her story straight when I bring her back to the Baron." Malcolm's eyes flicked to the skies and then back down quickly. Beth could tell he had no desire to be caught out here through another cyclone or worse.

The woman who seemed to be in charge gestured to the templar's weapon. "Where'd you get firepower like that, anyway? I thought the Barons kept that sort of technology for themselves and let the rest of their people suffer with crude tools?"

Something she said hit a nerve with the old templar. "The Baron's word is the word of the God Stripe. She doesn't need to justify herself to the masses." He looked a little more intently down the long barrel of the weapon. "And I just happen to be blessed enough to be able to . . . borrow a God-sent artifact when the Baron deems it necessary."

The woman laughed. Despite the weapon of destruction pointed in their general direction, Beth could see smirks on the faces of the other mainlanders, as well. Sly, on the other hand, just shook her head. "Take it easy on him. He doesn't know any better. None of them do."

"God-sent artifact, huh? Is that what the latest Baron is

still feeding you? How many generations of your people will go on believing those fairy tales before you all snap out of it?"

Portia turned to Beth. "B . . . what are they talking about?"

"No idea, but it sounds like maybe I'm not the only nonbeliever out here."

Portia shook her head. "Great. So you're religiously aligned with the cursed mainlanders. Congratulations."

"You don't have to live in the dark, you know? We can give you real answers. About what that is." The leader pointed up to the God Stripe.

Malcolm raised the weapon level with the woman's head. "I won't listen to blasphemy, mainlander. You won't turn me against the Baron or the God Stripe."

The woman shook her head in disappointment. "I'm not trying to convert or corrupt anyone. The Baron and her followers are welcome to live out there on your rocks and suffer through the hurricanes and fish diets until the end of time if that's what makes you all happy." She then gestured to the backpack. "But when those remnants of the old world fall from the sky, she doesn't have some God-spoken right to them. We live on this world, too. And we need all the help we can get."

"The God Rocks are gifts for the Bar—" Before Malcolm could finish his sentence, an arrow ripped through his calf, and he dropped to the ground. While his concentration was back on the bag, one of the archers managed to get off a quick shot. He screamed out in pain and dropped to one knee as he began opening fire. Beth slammed the hatch shut, and she and Portia disappeared back inside.

CHAPTER 59

SLY

And how many children of yours have been sent away to the islands, Tulip?

—The case of *Moira Vex v. The Council of War*, objection to the council's closing statements (struck from the official record)

As she rolled away from the blasts of fire from Malcolm's weapon and desperately tried to find cover on the open plateau, Sly thought about how far this was from what she wanted. She didn't want her tribe to be hurt, she didn't want Malcolm to be hurt—she didn't even want Radcliffe to be hurt. But somehow everything had gone to depths as the islanders would say.

Her mission was clear, even if it wasn't simple: Live among the islanders. Become a templar recruit. Pledge to Templar Malcolm, who was the only active templar the current Baron trusted with God Rock retrievals. If a God Rock came crashing down closer to the islands than to her homelands, intercept the retrieval and disappear with the package. She'd waited years for the opportunity. A meteor—or a God Rock as the islanders called it—wasn't just a chance to do what she'd been trained for since her youth, it was a chance to get back to her people. Infiltrations were always meant to be one-way tickets with only the slightest chance of ever making it home. Returning to the homelands with anything less than a meteor or some other priceless and life-changing artifact was unacceptable.

But she'd done it. And she was still a relative youth in the grand scheme of things. If Malcolm hadn't crawled out of his hiding spot with the most powerful artifact she'd ever seen, she could've been on her way back to the homelands by now. She could see her mother again. Would she recognize her after all these years? She'd grown so much since she'd been smuggled onto Charlie.

None of that mattered if she didn't survive, though. She raised her head up long enough to see Templar Malcolm holding his weapon with one hand and reaching to his wound with the other. He was firing off wild shots. The weapon was clearly meant to be aimed with two hands, but the opposing team of mainlanders were closing in on him. She risked standing up, but stayed crouched down so she could quickly dive out of the way if he pointed that thing in her direction again. She took a step forward with the intent to talk Malcolm down. Everything he knew about her may be a lie, but she still felt like it was possible that he didn't really want to hurt her. Everyone could walk away from this in one piece.

As she shifted her weight forward to move in with the rest of the team, she felt a hand grip her neck and pull her backward. The next thing she knew, she was being dragged down, and the sound of a heavy door slamming closed thudded over her head. She was lost in darkness for a moment until a torch was shoved in front of her face and she saw the heretics. She considered springing forward at them, but the curly-haired woman was armed with Templar Malcolm's sword, and despite her small frame, she actually looked ready to swing if she felt the need.

The low-island scavenger without the sword knelt down and spoke first. "Right. I think we ought to have a chat while they sort things out up above."

Chapter 60

Malcolm

We are the last barrier between the wild and the Chain. Between the cursed and the blessed.

—Proverbs of Templar Amaryte

The fight was lost. Malcolm knew his way around an encounter enough to see that much. The cursed mainlanders were closing in on him, and despite his superior weapon, he was losing blood and strength quickly. A second arrow had connected with his arm, and he felt sure the next projectile to break through his armor would likely be fatal. He had always told himself he would never be taken alive again. He'd learned from his mistakes. He would go down fighting if he ever found himself facing off against mainlanders again. But once he was back in the same situation, with death and the Depth Judgments in sight, he didn't feel ready to die. His chances were better if he stopped fighting. He could always escape later. He'd done it before. There would be a rescue team. It felt like ages had passed since they lit the signal fire in the swamps. He just had to buy time. Help would be on the way—Tamiyo wouldn't leave him out here to die. She still cared about him. He was sure of it.

So he lowered his weapon.

The remaining bow-wielding mainlanders raised their arrows and prepared to let loose. "WAIT!" Malcolm shouted. "I surrender. Don't fire."

The woman in charge approached Malcolm and kicked the weapon out of his reach. She took a knee in front of him, close enough that he could reach out and strike her down if the scavengers hadn't stripped him of the dagger he kept hidden in his belt. "You just shot down two of my friends." She pointed to a woman who wasn't moving on the ground. "Keelin was my cousin. You'll pay for their lives with yours, Templar." She spat out the last word as she drew a blade of her own from her belt.

"Wait." The pain and blood loss were catching up with Malcolm as the adrenaline of the fight faded. He was more seriously hurt than he had realized. "I know the Baron's secrets. Better than anyone. Where she stores everything. What the artifacts are capable of. How it all works." They had no way to know what was true. He just needed to buy time. "I'll . . . tell you everything," he managed to finish the thought before passing out.

Chapter 61

Beth

The templars have grown more savage than ever without a Baron to hold the leash.

—From the journal of Aphra of Alpha, Colonel of the Truthkeepers

"How many years have you been on the islands? How did you fake your identity to pass as part of a Charlie dynasty? Where do your people live?" Portia couldn't contain herself. Beth was sure Portia would have had a notebook out so she could write an accurate transcript of everything Sly had to say had it not been so dark in the tunnel.

Sly began to shake her head in annoyance, but Beth jumped in before she could refuse to answer. "Listen. I know we don't have a lot of time here. And we aren't looking to get caught in the middle of whatever is happening up there. The God Rock is yours. Your people can keep it."

"Ok . . ." Sly waited for the catch.

"But what's the truth she was talking about? About the God Stripe and the Baron and the islanders living in the dark . . . What don't we know? What is she hiding from us, Sly? Please." Beth thought of her mother again. Could she use whatever Sly knew to finally get her revenge? To turn the Chain against Tamiyo the Cruel?

Sly shifted uncomfortably. "It's . . . it's not my place to say. That's not part of my mission. You weren't supposed to hear any of that."

"Well, we did," Portia said as she pointed the tip of the sword toward the ground and leaned on the hilt. "Can't get that fish back off the hook."

"Sly, please. We have a right to know the truth. If we were lied to about it being impossible to live out here on the mainland, that's enough to change everything. But if there's more, we need to know. I need to know," Beth pleaded.

"The God Stripe . . . it's not what you think it is. You've built your whole lives around it. You think it sends gifts to your Barons and weapons to its chosen templars. But it's not a god. It's so far from that . . ."

"You're telling us that you know for a fact that the God Stripe isn't a god. So you're just a bunch of non-believers. Is that information supposed to impress us?" Portia asked, almost disappointed.

"It's not just that the stripe isn't a God, it's what the stripe *is*. We know. The Baron knows. Everyone knew at one time. But . . . the old Barons, they hid it from you. To make you worship them. There weren't a lot of resources to go around, so they wanted them for just the highest class families. The medicine, the technology, the weapons. The knowledge. They hid it all on that top island. It's all there under the Baron's tower."

"So if you know what the stripe is . . . then what is she hiding, Sly? Stop dancing around it." Beth leaned in close.

"It's the people who got away. Our ancestors. Not just the mainlanders, but all of our ancestors."

The color drained from Beth's face. Portia took a knee in front of Sly. She still held on to the hilt of the sword, but she was no longer in as threatening of a posture.

"What people? The people who got away from what?"

"Hundreds of years ago, humans came to this planet because we thought it was safe. We all used to live somewhere else. Incredibly far away. But we destroyed that planet. So we found the closest planet we could that seemed like it would be safe for us. This planet, where we live now, is very similar to our old home. But they wanted to be sure it was really safe. So not everyone landed right away. Instead, they sent down some scouting parties. And when they didn't die right away, they sent down some builders. And when they didn't die either, they sent down some scientists."

"Sent down? From where?" Portia asked, looking up at the hatch above them all.

"The stripe. It's not really one big stripe like it looks from down here. It's a bunch of smaller vehicles and pieces. All close to each other and circling around the planet together." She made a fist to represent the planet and used her other hand to draw a ring circling around it again and again.

"You're telling me . . . the God Stripe was full of people? It was like . . . some kind of floating settlement up there? In the striping skies?"

"No, I'm saying it *is* full of people. It *is* a floating settlement up there. Present tense," Sly answered. "Things went smoothly at first, but then the storms came. And the people weren't prepared. And the animals fought back a lot harder than the ones on our old planet did. So people were scared to come down. Living here is dangerous, right? Whether you're on the islands or the mainland. This planet isn't an easy life. And up there . . ." Now Sly looked up to the hatch. "Well the most powerful people in the stripe had grown pretty comfortable in their floating settlement. But there were only so many resources up there. So, they started sending the lower classes down here. To fend for themselves. They abandoned us. But we've all survived a lot longer than they expected I think."

"Why would the Baron want to hide that from us? What does she get out of the lie?" Beth was angry. She suspected she already knew the answer.

"Because the people up in those towers on Delta are greedy. The fewer people who know the truth, the more resources there are for the people on the upper island. The more comfort. The more power. And that's how the Baron and everyone else on Delta control the lives of everyone down to Alpha."

"But the Baron is selected at random." Beth thought of her sister again. "They're not just some descendants from a royal line."

"Right. Why give a stranger from Alpha all of that power? All of those secrets?" Portia asked.

"Everyone else on the island controls the Baron. She's a figurehead. She may feel like she's in charge, but the next Heir is already being groomed by the advisers and handmaidens as we speak. If the Baron steps far enough out of line, there's a new leader waiting to take her place. Barons are disposable to them. Just like everyone else. It's the advisers, the maids. They're pulling the strings."

Beth's anger turned to betrayal and sadness as she saw the guilt in Sly's eyes. "Why . . . why wouldn't you tell us? Why wouldn't someone striping tell us?!"

Sly shook her head. "It's just not that simple. There's history between our people. Wars. Thousands of lives lost on both sides. There was a treaty eventually. An agreement to stay out of each other's way. Promises were made that we wouldn't interfere."

"Well you're clearly not out of the way now. What changed?" Portia asked.

"The rocks. The meteors. They started falling more frequently. We don't know who's sending them down, but we need them. She can't just take them all anymore."

"What are they?" Portia asked.

"It's different every time. Weapons, medicine, information. Things we need. Things everyone here needs. It's not fair of the Baron to send out her templars to steal them all and then just bury them in her tower for a rainy day. Whoever is sending them wants the people to have them. We've tried to contact them up there, but that sort of communication requires tools that are probably all hidden under your Baron's tower."

"If you had just told us . . ." Beth started.

"What? You'd overthrow her? You'd leave the islands? She must have an arsenal on Delta at this point. You bottom islanders wouldn't stand a chance against her. She's too powerful. And you weren't raised for the mainland. It's been just two days, and you've almost died a half dozen times. You wouldn't last a month."

"Stripe that. You should've told us." Beth stood up. "We're getting out of here. I don't want to see you again, Sly."

"The feeling is mutual. And . . . I'm sorry. We have a code. I couldn't—"

"The templars have a code, too. People love having something to excuse their awful behavior, huh?" Beth started to climb the ladder again.

Portia slid the sword back through her belt and looked at Sly. "What about this place? Do you know what the depths it is?"

"Some of those first people that came down had the bright

idea they could get back to the stripe once things started going to hell. This place, and other places like it, have something to do with that. Making it so the trip down from the stripe wasn't just a one-way deal."

"Did they?" Portia asked as she started to climb.

Sly didn't sound confident. "I don't know, honestly. Nobody is left who understands how this stuff works, though. So, it's as good as useless now . . . but somebody up there is sending stuff down for us. I like to think maybe someone did make it back up there. And they haven't forgotten about the people they left behind down here."

Chapter 62

Sly

I may fail to convince you today, but a new generation is rising. And they will burn our traditions to the ground.

—The case of *Moira Vex v. The Council of War*, closing statements

As they climbed the ladder, Sly wondered what her tribe would do with these two. Setting them free after everything they'd seen would break nearly every rule of the treaty. Templars? Sure, they could be trusted with a secret or two. But a couple of low islanders? If they made it back to their island it could destroy generations of lies and secrets. That wasn't really Sly's problem, but if the stories of the old wars were true, then the treaty was best for everyone.

Beth swung the hatch open, and they all looked up to find the surviving pack of mainlanders waiting for them.

"Tulip." Sly smiled up at the leader of the group, who was

extending a hand to help her out of the hole. "Thanks for waiting for me."

Once she was topside, Sly quickly spotted Malcolm unconscious and bound. "Managed to take him alive. What's the plan, then?" She breathed a sigh of relief that the old templar hadn't been put down. He was in for a hell of a questioning, but once they made it back to their homelands they wouldn't kill him unless they had to.

"Oh, don't worry about him. The details he's going to share about the current Baron and her operations will keep him alive for years when we get him back home. Let's talk about these two, though." She pointed Malcolm's weapon of destruction at Beth and Portia, who instinctively ducked their heads out of its path.

"Right." Sly considered how much to reveal about what she had shared with them. "They're low-born scavengers. Might have some island underworld connections we could use if we keep them in play." She wasn't sure why she was vouching for them. Or why she was feeling sorry about Radcliffe or Malcolm or any of them. She had her own people to return to now, but she didn't relish the thought of hurting the islanders. She just wanted to get home. It was so close now.

"Keep us in play?" Beth asked. One of the mainlanders—Sly didn't know her name—started to move forward to collect their weapons, and Portia's grip on the sword's hilt tightened.

"Hang on, let's all slow down and think about this!" Sly found herself stepping in to protect Beth and Portia.

"New assets in the field would be useful. Especially ones with connections. It's a good instinct," Tulip started. Sly could tell there was more coming, though. "But they've seen too much. They could compromise the treaty."

"We can keep our mouths shut," Beth chimed in. "It's

basically what we do for a living. Nobody ever has to know what happened out here."

"And you'll help us smuggle mainlanders onto and off the islands? Risk your own lives for a cause you know nothing about and will never understand?" Tulip asked.

Portia and Beth looked at each other and came to some kind of silent agreement that only two people who had known each other for a lifetime could do. It was a phenomenon Sly had never had the honor of being half of.

Portia spoke for both of them. "We have no allegiance to the Baron. And we're in the business of staying alive. You can trust our word. We'll do whatever you need if it means we walk away from this plateau alive and unbound."

Tulip looked at Sly. "You truly think we can trust them?"

Again, Sly wasn't really sure why she felt bargaining for their lives was worth the risk. Maybe she'd just seen enough death for one day. "We can trust them. They're criminals and heretics, but they've got no love for the Baron and the rest of the royalty. And they seem to know their way on and off the islands well enough."

Tulip smiled at the pair. "Guess it's your lucky day then, friends."

Sly let out a breath of relief. "So we cut them loose and haul the templar back to the homelands. Best to get a move on before the next twister races through, right?"

Tulip rested a hand on Sly's shoulder, and the spy shuddered just a bit as she thought back to Templar Malcolm comforting her in that same way. "You've done good work here, Sylva. We've got the gift from the Stripe, a new templar informant, and two additional smugglers in our network. The leaders are going to be very pleased with your work."

"I look forward to meeting with them again after all of this time," Sly responded. "And with my mother. Is she well?"

Tulip's grasp on Sly's shoulder tightened a bit.

"There's more work to be done here, Sylva. With the templar in custody, you have the potential to control the narrative." Tulip gestured to the weapon on Portia's hip. "You head back to the Baron with that sword, half of the scraps from the rock that we can spare, and a story about cyclones and giant lizards, and you'll be a hero. The lone survivor of the retrieval team. You could ascend to templar for this. Imagine your proximity to the Baron then! You'll be the most valuable informant in the history of the network."

"But . . . *this* was my mission." Sly pointed to the bag slung around Tulip's torso. "Not to become a templar. Not to stay on the islands forever. I've done what the leaders sent me out to do."

"And you've done it well, child. But this opportunity . . . it's too grand to pass up. To have a mainlander in the Baron's circle of templars is unheard of. And nobody is saying it's forever. The leaders will recognize your sacrifice and relieve you of your duty once you've gathered enough intel."

"No. This isn't how this is supposed to happen, Tulip. I'm done. I'm ready to go home."

Tulip's hand released Sly's shoulder. "I'm sorry, child. This is an order. You're going back to the islands. Take the scavengers with you."

Tulip turned around and began splitting up the God Rock treasure into two bags. She handed one to Sly and seemed too ashamed to meet her eyes. "Your mother is well, niece. I'll tell her of your victory here."

CHAPTER 63

JONAH

My watch has ended. May the God Stripe's light guide your heart.

—Excerpt from the departure letter of Lord Drolt, Senior Adviser to Baron Agrius

The impact site of the God Rock was larger than Jonah remembered from his days working on retrieval crews. The trail leading to where the God Rock had crashed down had been mostly destroyed, likely by a storm that raged through, but the crater was hard to miss. He made his way across the plateau landing and kneeled down next to the empty crater. He was surprised to find that the crater point wasn't the most interesting thing there. The crash site was littered with the remnants of a battle. Any fallen fighters had been removed from the area, but fresh blood still pooled on the dirt.

The good news was that Malcolm's body was nowhere to be seen. That meant the mainlanders may have kept him alive

... again. Jonah pulled his looking glasses from his bag and began scanning the horizon for signs of a group riding away from the plateau and farther inland. It didn't take him long to spot them. He shoved the glasses back into his pack and set off after them.

He recited his Oaths as he sprinted further away from the safety of his tower in the Chain and deeper into the Land God's domain.

Chapter 64

Sly

My daughter made me a promise before she left. I go to sleep every night wishing it could come true.

—The case of *Moira Vex v. The Council of War*, closing statements

Sly, Beth, and Portia covered the distance to the swamps in near silence. Sly's head was still spinning from Tulip's orders. The idea of going home was all that had driven her through her training years and her time on Templar Malcolm's crew. The lies were growing old. She could barely remember who she had been before her time on the islands began. She needed to get home. Get back to her family, before she had lost herself entirely.

And if Baron Tamiyo really did make her a templar? The network would never let her go home then. An asset that close to the Baron was too valuable to just give up. And templars served the Baron for life, even after they retired their swords. She knew what this mission meant. She was never going home.

"So, Templar Sly, huh? Doesn't quite have a formal ring to it, in my opinion. Wonder if they'll rename you for the position." Beth broke the silence as they were hiking across a particularly muddy portion of the swamp.

"Sylva. Sly is just . . . a nickname, I guess. My real name is Sylva."

"Well Templar Sylva, that's a different story. Bards could really do something with that one. And your tale of single-handedly recovering a God Rock and slaying a wyvern. What do you think, Portia?"

"You'll make a fine templar, Sly. If that's what you want to do," Portia replied, mostly under her breath.

"If that's what I *want* to do?" Sly snapped back. "I'm not exactly being given a choice here, in case you missed the 'direct order' part of the conversation."

Portia looked from Beth to Sly. "We all have a choice."

Sly shook her head in frustration. "You don't get it. I can't just go back home without following my orders. They won't take me in. You don't know what it's like to have to play by the rules. You're just a couple of—"

Portia finished the thought for her. "Criminals? Heretics? Low-island scrappers?"

Sly shook her head. "I'm not trying to insult you, but it's true. You just do whatever you want, and as long as you stay under the radar, there aren't any consequences. I can't just go back and abandon my mission. I'd be an outcast."

Beth chimed in. "Well . . . what if there was a middle ground? You don't go back home *yet*, but the situation on the islands changes enough that your mission is over."

"Templars serve the Baron for life, Beth," Sly said in defeat. "Once I go back and hand this over," she patted the bag on her back, "it's over."

"That's why you aren't going to go back and hand it over." Beth smirked. "You're going to give it to us."

Chapter 65

Malcolm

Death for the God Stripe, the Baron, or a fellow templar is the only honorable end.

—Proverbs of Templar Amaryte

The sound of a fire crackling woke Malcolm from a hazy sleep. He slowly blinked his eyes open as memories started to rush back to him in blurry fragments. Being surrounded on the plateau. Being dragged across the plains on some kind of sled. And then waking up to this. He had no idea how much time he had lost. The sun had fallen and the God Stripe was glowing overhead, so he hoped it had only been a few hours and not a whole day.

Malcolm tried not to fidget as he assessed the environment. The fire was just about ten feet in front of him, and he saw two mainlanders passed out next to it. There was a tent nearby, and he assumed a few others were sleeping in there. Footsteps paced back and forth from somewhere behind him, which he assumed belonged to at least one guard.

He weighed his options as he lay there trying to calm his

heart and slow his breathing. He concentrated on the fire. Looking at the massive bright sky up above was making his head spin. The fire was small and contained, though. He focused there to clear his mind. The old templar wasn't sure how he could pull it off, but he knew he needed to get back to the islands. He simply wasn't built for all of this space.

Malcolm found himself worrying that the rescue party should've arrived already . . . if they were coming. He was certain Tamiyo would send one, but would they track this far inland just to find one missing squad member? If Radcliffe had successfully gotten the God Rock back to them, there was the chance they might consider that victory enough. If he had still been at the crash site, that was one thing. They would certainly have gone that far looking for signs of him. But searching beyond the plateau was incredibly dangerous. They would risk losing a whole other team to cyclones and mainlander attacks just for one templar. He knew it wasn't worth it. He was on his own.

His hand bindings were tight, but his legs were free. Perhaps they weren't as worried about him escaping while he was entirely unconscious. So he could run, but how far would he make it? The guard's pacing seemed to have stopped, and Malcolm risked rolling over to see if he might have an opening. If he had a chance to run now, he had to take it. He wouldn't be dragged back to their homelands and taken prisoner for life.

He found the guard just a few feet away with her back turned toward the fire. She was staring out into the darkness and her body language told Malcolm that she was squinting to make out something in the dark. Maybe she had heard some kind of noise out there? Maybe the same noise had been whatever had woken Malcolm a moment earlier.

Malcolm stayed frozen in place, watching the guard. He didn't dare make a break for it with the guard so close, even if she did seem to be distracted. The aging templar would need a bigger head start than this. The guard took a step forward and drew a dagger from her belt—a steel blade a little longer than the length of an adult's hand. The kind of thing nobody but a templar would ever have access to on the Chain, but out here a lowly guard carried one around like it was nothing. Malcolm still didn't hear or see anything in the darkness.

Suddenly, and seemingly out of nowhere, a flash of steel caught the reflection of the fire as it swung down and cut through the guard's torso. The mainlander let out a cry as she fell, but it was too late for backup to help. There was no recovery from a wound that deep. Malcolm sprung to his feet before the guard's body had even hit the ground. He raced over to meet whoever was wielding the blade and held out his bound hands.

When he got close enough to see Jonah's face illuminated by the firelight, he instinctively pulled back. "What the stripe are you doing here?" he whispered, despite the fact that the whole camp was already stirring behind him. There was no chance of getting away quietly now.

"Your bindings, Malcolm!" Jonah held out the blade toward him. Malcolm still shied back. He honestly wasn't sure who he trusted less, the mainlanders or his old brother. "I can't take them all on my own. We'll need your hands!"

The mainlanders by the fire were up and scrambling for their weapons, and Malcolm saw movement coming from the tents as well. His eyes darted around the camp until he found what he was looking for. His God-sent artifact was leaning on a pole up against the tent. He had to get to it before they did if there was any chance of survival. He looked back to Jonah in desperation.

His old friend pleaded. "Please. You can trust me. I won't run. Not this time."

Malcolm held out his hands and pulled the bindings apart

to create space between them. Jonah struck down and sliced straight through the ropes.

"Follow me," he barked at Jonah and prayed to the God Stripe that the retired templar still had the nerve to charge forward into battle.

Without a moment's hesitation, the two old friends dashed across the camp toward the tent. The mainlanders by the fire were fully armed at this point, and Jonah stepped in to cut them off as they tried to intercept Malcolm's path. Jonah began hacking away at one of their spears with his superior weapon, while Malcolm charged into the other soldier with his head low and drove them toward the fire with his shoulders. At the last moment Malcolm lifted the mainlander up over his head and tossed her onto the burning coals. He lost no speed as he leaped over the burning mainlander and the fire as he carried on toward the tent.

Malcolm reached the tent just in time to find Tulip emerging and reaching for the weapon. He was completely unarmed and would be torn apart once she leveled it at him. He let his adrenaline lead him as he dove forward and placed one hand on the weapon. He was on the ground, pulling the artifact toward him, but she had the upper hand. She had two hands on the artifact and was winning the tug-of-war.

Malcolm hung on to the weapon with all of his might as Tulip raised a boot and prepared to stomp down on his face. Before she could deliver the blow, Jonah charged in and slammed the hilt of his sword into her face. Tulip reflexively reached for her bloody nose with both hands and reeled back into the tent. The weapon flew down and smacked Malcolm in the chest now that the resistance was gone.

He lost his breath for a moment, but he sprang up to his feet and stood shoulder to shoulder with Jonah as they assessed the remaining forces in the camp.

"Orders, Templar Malcolm?" Jonah asked.

Malcolm couldn't help but smirk at his old friend. The years of resentment, anger, and disappointment were fading away in the fog of relief and adrenaline. They might grow back and return if the pair could make it out of this mess, but for now he was just happy to have a friend out here in the middle of the cursed plains.

"No survivors," Malcolm snarled back.

"For the God Stripe!" Jonah cried out as he raised his sword up into an aggressive battle stance.

"For the Baron!" Malcolm shouted back in reply as they began to tear through the rest of the camp.

Chapter 66

Sly

I miss her as much as the day you dragged her away.

—The case of *Moira Vex v. The Council of War*, parting words

Sly couldn't openly disobey a direct order, but she didn't have to protect the treaty anymore. Beth's plan could work. It had to work. She wouldn't let Tulip stop her from getting back home.

After they'd come to an agreement, Sly split away from Beth and Portia and began hiking toward the spot where she'd left Radcliffe, Simone, and Arin. The trio of recruits were the last loose thread Sly figured she would need to tie up to get her story straight and be able to get back on the islands without any suspicion.

She reached the clearing and found nothing but grass and mud in the place where she'd left the three recruits. She knelt down in the grass and didn't find any blood or clear signs of a struggle. That meant the group had likely woken up before a wyvern or giant lizard happened to come across them. She was thinking about what her next steps would be when she heard a stick crack on the ground behind her.

She twirled around and drew her weapon to find Simone, Arin, and Radcliffe standing over her. She was grossly outnumbered. That was fine. She had prepared for this. She dropped her weapon to her side and breathed a sigh of relief.

"Thank the God Stripe. You're all alive."

Radcliffe leveled his weapon a bit higher and scowled at Sly. "Where. Is. The. God. Rock?"

"The . . . the scavengers came for it. Don't you remember being ambushed?" She started to get to her feet, but Radcliffe stepped forward with his weapon and directed her back to the ground.

Arin spoke up first. "We didn't see who attacked us."

Simone chimed in behind him. "But we woke up in this clearing, and you and the God Rock were the only things missing. Bit suspicious, wouldn't you say?"

"And you think I somehow overpowered the three of you and stole it? Are you striping crazy? Why would I do that?" Sly shot back.

"Enough," Radcliffe cut in. "They don't remember anything, Sly, but I do. I remember you. Pushing me through a clearing. And I saw them, knocked out, and the next thing I knew I was waking up in here."

"Because I was running from them, Cliffe! I didn't know Simone and Arin were here. I was as surprised as you to find them back here."

"Then why didn't you wake up with the rest of us?" Simone shouted.

Sly took a breath. "They wanted to question one of us, I guess. They took the pack off Radcliffe and dragged me away kicking and screaming. They set up camp for the night, and I was able to slip away after they all passed out. I ran back here as fast as I could. But they're going to realize I'm gone sooner than later. We need to move."

"You've been lying to us since the beginning, Sly. I'm not falling for it again."

"Oh yeah? Then why did I come back here to try and find you all? Who beat the depths out of me and ruined my face? And more importantly, where's the striping God Rock?"

Simone and Arin glanced at each other and then lowered their weapons. Sly breathed a sigh of relief. Radcliffe only scowled even harder.

"No. Don't do this. Don't believe her," he growled.

Arin set a reassuring hand on his shoulder. "Come on, Cliffe. She's right. If she stole the God Rock, then where is it?"

Chapter 67
Beth

For Beth — My sister. The Truthbringer. The traitor. And the new world she gave to us.

—Final journal entry of Aphra of Alpha, Colonel of the Truthkeepers

The bag of remnants from the God Rock—or *meteorite* as Sly had called it—lay on the floor of the boat as Beth and Portia sailed back toward the islands under the light of the God Stripe and the stars. Beth looked down at the salvaged treasure for a moment and then smiled at Portia.

"Bag full of artifacts sitting at your feet and you haven't so much as cracked it open to take a peek yet. It's like I don't even know you anymore."

Portia kicked the bag and looked out at the calm waters illuminated by the light of the clear sky and the reflection from the God Stripe. "Does it even matter anymore? All the artifacts we've ever found. The books, the tools, they're just the tip of the iceberg. With what we know now, I don't get how we go back to normal."

Beth shook her head. "So what if we don't?"

"We don't what?"

"Go back to normal. *Stripe* normal." Beth smiled wider.

"Even if we did try to tell people what we learned, nobody would believe us. Why should they? It sounds insane. If I hadn't seen that tunnel for myself, seen Sly's people. . . I don't think I could've wrapped my head around it." Portia shook her head. "It's too big a lie. We'd be asking people to forget everything they know about where we came from, our God, our whole striping planet. How do you tell someone their whole life is a lie?" Portia asked.

Beth kicked the bag toward Portia. "You start small."

Portia looked at the bag and then back to Beth. "And you think that would work?"

Beth looked out across the water toward the islands where she had lived her whole life. "I think you're right that the whole story is too much to swallow at once. But piece by piece? The idea of the Baron and everyone else up on Delta lying to us isn't that far-fetched. So we just reveal one lie at a time. The weapons. The tech. The medicine. The mainlanders. And then, eventually . . ." Beth's gaze wandered from the islands up to the God Stripe, and she thought for a moment. "Eventually, people will have heard enough to be ready to learn about them."

"They'll kill us if we talk to the wrong person. Or if the rumors get traced back to us. This is . . . a level of heresy that is crossing a line even for us." Beth knew the risks already, but Portia still felt like she had to say them out loud.

"You're right. We could just keep our mouths shut. Go back to business as usual. Try to forget everything we know. Depths, now that we know the mainland is habitable, we could sail up the coast, find a place just for the two of us. Leave the Chain to Mitch, the Baron, and all those other monsters. Say the word, and I'm there with you. Either option. I know none of this is going to bring my mother back from the depths. Or save my sister from her fate." Beth meant it this time. She was done chasing treasure. Done dreaming about revenge against the throne. Done living for the hunt. She knew the truth, and Portia had survived. She could call it quits here and consider this a victory.

"But it would be wrong, wouldn't it?" Portia stood up beside Beth and looked out to the islands with her. She still wore Malcolm's sword on her hip, and she was growing to like the weight and security it brought with it.

"I don't want to drag you into something this dangerous unless you really want it," Beth reassured her. "Seriously. A quiet life up the coast is just waiting for us. You can scare off any long wyverns that bother us with your new toy." Beth nodded to the sword.

"I think a quiet life up the coast will still be there waiting for us after we stir up a little rebellion." Portia smiled back at Beth for a moment before moving her gaze toward the islands. "Let's go home."

Epilogue

I hope when my days are numbered, and the secrets are yours, you carry them as well as those who came before you.

—Handmaiden's transcript of recurring conflict resolution meetings between Baron Agrius and the Heir, final meeting

On occasion, the Heir had the opportunity to visit the lower islands and observe life among her future subjects. According to her handmaidens, this was one of her most important lessons. It was vital she learned what life on each island was like and understood the purpose of each piece of the Chain's workforce; how it played into the overall economy and prosperity of their society as a whole.

This was a concept the Heir never really found all that complicated, but she still didn't mind the excuse to visit somewhere outside Delta and its high walls once in a while. Her books and lessons explained each island's primary exports and duties very clearly, so she had never really understood what sitting in the marketplace on Charlie or idling outside a factory on Beta was supposed to teach her. She tried to be a good student, though, and went along with her escort through the motions.

The Heirs were paraded through the streets as an infant when they were selected by the Baron, but afterwards they were always kept out of public view until their own ascension. They were never put in any position to potentially overshadow the sitting Baron. That meant she was able to roam the other islands, with escorts obviously, without any fear of being recognized for who she was. It was during one of these lessons when she first realized something was different on the lower islands. Something had changed since her last visit.

She was walking through a crowded market district in the stacks of Beta when she first saw a symbol carved onto a stack a few stories up from the ground level. The markings were unfamiliar to her, but seemed to be a T, B, and L interwoven together. She found it quite aesthetically pleasing and wanted to take out a notebook and copy the markings down so she could remember it.

The Heir tugged at her handmaiden's cloak and pointed up to the symbols. "Madam. What is that?"

"Ah, you know how things can be in these slums, child. Heretical street art. Depths will judge the savages when their time comes." The Heir was surprised at the harsh reaction. Street drawings seemed fairly common down here on the lower islands, and she didn't realize it was such a serious crime against the God Stripe. She looked to the sky, wondering how Maiden Lydia, or anyone, could know what did and what didn't offend the God Stripe.

Her handmaiden pushed her along before she could get her notebook out, and the Heir quickly found herself being nudged into a crowded shop farther down the alley.

"Take a few moments and look around, my child. This seems like a good place to rest a bit until the crowd dies down out there." Her escort began examining some sculptures carved from sea glass that were hanging just inside the door.

The Heir stepped farther into the shop and found herself browsing through an album of art. The drawings weren't the best she'd ever seen, but they were impressive for a lower islander. As she understood it, they worked very long hours on these islands and there wasn't any time to dedicate to the arts. The subjects were mostly boats and the ocean, but there were a few more exciting pieces with wyverns and even one with a rendering of a giant squid. She found herself grinning as she thumbed through the pieces.

The shopkeeper, a middle-aged man with a limp, walked over and smiled at the Heir. She returned the gesture. "These are very lovely, Sir."

"Why thank you, young lady." His smile grew a bit wider and he leaned over the counter to look at the work alongside her. "Not many customers find those very interesting, to be honest with you."

She stopped on a drawing of a massive sea beast breaching the surface of the ocean. "Are they from your imagination?"

He looked closer and chuckled. "Afraid not. I was a Depth Walker when I was a bit closer to your age." He patted the leg that had been dragging a bit behind the other when he was walking. "Forced into early retirement, but while I was out there . . . well, you'd be surprised how much time is spent just sitting in boats and staring out at the sea. Plenty of time to draw. Or sew. Or whatever it is you do to pass the time."

She flipped the page of the portfolio again and found herself looking at a massive water cyclone towering over ships that rocked on massive waves. She was speechless.

"Ah." He reached across and tapped the drawing with his hand. "That's the one that ruined my leg. Drew it up while I was stuck in the healing tents for a few moons."

While he was gesturing at the drawing, she spotted the instantly recognizable bottom corner of the pattern poking out from under his sleeve. After a quick glance to her handmaiden to make sure she wasn't watching too closely, she reached out and grabbed his hand and pointed.

She lowered her voice. "I've seen this before. It's the art from the stacks, right?"

The shopkeeper chuckled as he pulled his long sleeve up a bit to reveal the rest of the ink tattoo on his right wrist. The intertwined letters were even more beautiful than they had been on the side of the stacks, and the Heir found herself smirking as if she was in on some secret only a few people knew.

She looked back to her handmaiden, who was taking a few pieces of coral off the rope to purchase and bring back to Delta. She turned to the shopkeeper and pointed at the tattoo once more. "What does it mean?"

This time it was him who looked to make sure the young girl's escort wasn't listening before he leaned across the counter and whispered in her ear, "The Baron Lies."

He pulled his sleeve back down, raised a finger to his lips, and gave a quiet "shush" before crossing the shop to help the handmaiden make her purchase.

Acknowledgments

Thank you to my editors, Patti Connolly and Jessica Filippi, who reviewed multiple drafts of this manuscript and provided invaluable feedback at every stage.

Thanks to Chris Olds, who was one of the first people to ever chat about Salvage with me. His maps and cover art perfectly capture the tone of this world and The God Stripe Saga wouldn't be the same without his collaboration.

I would also like to thank Kate Hoffman, Sadie Buckallew, Sophia Glock, Jarod Roselló, Melanie Hooyenga, Dave Housley, John McComas, and James Leavy for all of their help, feedback, and support as this project came together.

www.ingramcontent.com/pod-product-compliance
Lightning Source LLC
Chambersburg PA
CBHW011908210125
20660CB00001B/1